I0626533

The Lure of Dangerous Women

The Lure of Dangerous Women

SHANNA GERMAIN

WAYZGOOSE PRESS

The Lure of Dangerous Women
Copyright © 2012 by Shanna Germain.

All rights reserved. No part of this publication may be repro-
duced, stored in or introduced into a retrieval system, or
transmitted, in any form, or by any means (electronic, mechanical, photocopying, recording, or otherwise) without the
prior written permission of the copyright owner.

ISBN-10: 1938757033
ISBN-13: 978-1-938757-03-7

Published in the United States by Wayzgoose Press.

Edited by Dorothy E. Zemach.
Cover design by DJ Rogers.
Book design by M. Cutajar.

This is a work of fiction. Names, characters, places, brands,
media, and incidents are either the product of the author's
imagination or are used fictitiously.

These stories first appeared in the following publications:

"Trill," Winner, *Anthology Builder Match-that-Cover Contest*,
2009
"Seed," *Subversion: Science Fiction & Fantasy Tales of Challeng-
ing the Norm*, 2011
"Seeing Stars," *Triangulation: Taking Flight*; 2008
"Forced Expiration," *Absinthe Literary Review*, 2006
"The Lure of Dangerous Women," *Blood Fruit*, 2010

For all of the dangerous women I know and love.

CONTENTS

TRILL

I NOTICED THE GIRL FIRST. How could I not? I am a man, if nothing else. Wheat-headed and sky-eyed, with a beautiful pink mouth always open in laughter or song. And then her brother. Twins, it seemed, differentiated only by their clothes and colors. Her in yellow, a skirt that swung 'round her ankles, doing nothing to hide her delicate-boned feet. Him in blue pants that would be too short by fall.

Some would say summer incarnate. Beauty perfected. I knew better. They were each saved from such clichés by a single and small error of the body. Hers was a mole at the corner of her eye; an ugly thing, too large for her face. It gave her features a one-sided downcast, as though she'd pushed too hard to be born, scrubbing her face against her mother's insides.

His was a tiny harelip, a slit cut in the middle of his upper lip, the pink skin pulled back to expose a sliver of teeth. It took his smile from the sweet petal of youth to something more knowing, nearly sinister.

It seems to me it is these tiny slips, these errors of some maker's judgment, that let us be whole in our imperfections. Much as music must never be so perfect that it goes unheard or unnoticed. There must always be some small hitch of breath, a murmur where there should be silence, a stilled pale where there should be a red beat of pulse.

———————◆——————

The children played every day in the small cemetery behind the inn where I stayed. I wasn't a traveler, no, although I'd gained that reputation by then. I lived there, I did. Born and raised, although I'd left and come back after many years. I was one of the town's own. If anyone chose to look, they would see my mother's grave marker sits in the cemetery still.

Days I'd stretch out on the grass, legs crossed at the ankle, leaning back beneath a big oak. In nearby house, small winged birds called their freedom to their family clipped inside window cages, and I put the flute to my lips to echo their call. I used a short, simple flute, made from elk bone. There were no elk in that part of the world, and the notes pearled from my lips, unbeckoning to any.

The twins noticed, but they didn't at the same time. I was just some man in the cemetery, another sound among many. I've heard hunters work this way, and animal tamers. Sitting still until they're part of the scenery, scent and sound and motion.

Still, the twins were curious. That was the key. That's always the key. A desire to know, to discover.

After a few weeks, I switched instruments. I carried the crimson case down to the garden, unwrapped the pale pinkish flute from its black velvet. This one longer, more intricate, the long hollow bone inlaid at one end with a dark braid around its surface. Through the years, my mouth and hands have worn the bone smooth, small indents where my fingers dance over the holes, a softness where my lips settle to breathe.

The boy was the first to come, intrigued, his lips curling. He was too young to understand, I think, what happened to his mouth when he smiled, and so he smiled freely. While he approached, she sat, leaning against a tilted grave marker taller than she, watching me without pretense, the patterns of leaves and sunlight spreading along her skin. From so far away, the mole was nearly impossible to see, and her beauty was marred only by that perfection. I wanted her closer, to see her as she truly was.

I could have acknowledged one or the other, but I merely kept playing, fingers dancing as my lips moved along the pale instrument, the material sheened and softened by years of playing, smooth as skin.

In the shy way that boys have, he circled far away, a moth unsure of the light, fluttering around as though the broken markers interested him, the broken twigs, the inn wall that edged against the cemetery. I kept playing, parting my lids enough to watch him. Coming ever closer, until finally, he was standing before me, kicking at a stone.

I played some more, no longer matching the bird songs, but taking them higher, slower. A lullaby and a morning song. Sleep and be awakened. I watched my fingers move over the instrument, not because I needed to but because children spook easily, like does or rabbits. You must let them approach while making them think you're unaware.

The boy, unable to keep his curiosity hidden, looked at me full on. I watched the split of his lip open and close as he spoke.

"How do you make that sound?"

Without ceasing my tune, I lifted the instrument higher, showed the places where my mouth moved along it. The tone changed, upbeat tempo, a danceable trill. Even the girl's feet stopped their ragged swinging against the wall, began to beat in time.

"I could teach you," I said, as the music died away. "Come tonight and I'll teach you."

———◆●◆———

It is easiest to start on a simple, hollow instrument. One or two holes for notes. Learning how to blow, move your breath through your chest. Rise. Fall. Space. Do it again.

"Everyone should have their own instrument," I told the boy as I leaned against the tree trunk. He hadn't come alone. His sister tagged along, always out of reach, always watching. She hung at edge of the shadows, swinging her dress around her thighs. Sometimes she popped her thumbnail in her mouth, ran her tongue along the edge of it.

"Something simple to start," I added.

"I like yours," he said. Petulant. Wanting. You could tell he'd been well taught, the way his fluttery hands tucked into his pockets so he couldn't grab.

I held the flute out on my palms as reward for his good manners. "You can touch it," I said. "But only the maker can play these flutes. They're... special."

It was true. How else to describe to these children what they were embarking upon, what learning experience awaited them? The same as my own, once, long ago.

"Do you want to make one? One for your very own?"

How could he resist such an offer? The boy nodded, sucked his lip. Behind me, the creatures moved in the dark confines of their metal cages. They made the same sound as the girl did when she twirled, her dress rustled against her thighs.

I looked at her, a careful look, from the corner of my eye. She wasn't moving closer. But I could tell by the pull of her face below her mole, the flicker of her gaze as it jumped from her brother to the flute to me, that she wasn't going away either.

"We'll make a simple one-note to start," I said. And the boy seemed pleased with that.

I brought the creatures forth, sleek and dark, fur like hematite. Teeth exploring with a nip, but not a bite. They wouldn't bite, of course, or run. Long tails slithering in the darkness. They were the biggest out of all that that had come. I'd kept one for each of us, and set the rest free. I am many things, but I am not a man of excess, no matter what they might say.

The boy didn't flinch and, I was pleased to see, neither did she. Merely leaned closer, bending at the waist the way girls do who wear dresses, thumbnail dragging along her pointed tongue.

The knife was tucked inside the flute case, and I pulled it out, laying the flute on the dark material, close at hand in case I needed it.

"It's very fast," I said, as I reached in and took one of the rats by the neck, sliding the knife across in one, slick movement. The boy winced slightly, maybe at the blood, maybe at the rat's final shudder against the grass before it went still. I wanted to look at the girl, but she was behind me, circled behind the tree. The sound of her footsteps was stilled, though, and I knew she was watching, learning. She could come to me in time.

I held the knife to the boy, hilt toward him, and nodded as he took it. His hands shook, but he seemed determined, squatting down next to the cage, eyeing the creatures.

"They won't hurt you," I said.

It was true.

"They're only rats."

This was true also.

He was a good student that first night. I explained the importance of quick death, paying homage to the creatures under our care. Despite his trepidation, he took the rat's life in a single movement. I nodded, pleased. "Tomorrow, I'll show you how to make your flute."

———◆•◆•◆———

The other lessons didn't go as well. Skinning, gathering the femur from the mess. He worked diligently, but he was hesitant, his hands clumsy, furrowing his brow and sucking air through his cleft so that it wheezed through his teeth.

And through it all, the girl watched, sometimes twirling around in her ever-present skirts. Sometimes staying still, crouched, nothing moving but her eyes. I knew she could hear me and I'd raise my voice just a little, enough to carry to her ears and no further. Even if she wasn't going to make a flute, I somehow felt it was important that she hear the lessons, that she have an understanding of what was being done.

Finally, the boy's flute was finished. A simple one-hole instrument – I couldn't bear to watch him try to carve anything more with his clumsy hands – but it would do. I pushed my fingers across a similar instrument of my own, but didn't breathe into it. They'd come for me, but he needed to bring them on his own.

"You do it," I said. "You call them."

They came, of course. They always do. They can't help it.

Lower forms are the easiest, of course. Rats and birds and bats make simple, boring prey. They come, seduced by the call. Enthralled. Cats and dogs are harder, but not by much. Easy enough to tame. They succumb, as they must, to the music and the music-maker. But children, oh, children are the hardest of all. Such complex, complicated brains. Curious, calculating, ever-expanding. Children must be beguiled and enticed. They must be left to decide on their own whether they will be seduced, and in what form, and to what degree.

The rats, simple creatures, streamed across the grass in a low dance of moving bodies and tails. Quiet beneath the music, settling around the boy. Waiting to see what he'd do, what he wanted of them.

"What do I do with 'em?"

I had to hold back a sigh. I'd hoped for more from this pupil. Perhaps I'd miscalculated, been swayed by their imperfect beauty, jumped too soon?

He sucked air in through his lip, and I leaned down and smiled to him, fingers playing along the pinkish flute in my fingers, but not putting it to my mouth.

"Whatever you like," I said. "Take them through

the gravestones, like a dance. They'll follow you."

And being given permission, or perhaps just the idea, he nodded. Put his lips to the tiny, one-holed flute and played a few notes. The rats shifted, moved around him in a swarm of one. Gaining confidence, he stood, still trilling his notes, walking backwards as though afraid to let them from his sight, and stepped between the graves, watching them swarm and circle in his footsteps. The creatures followed, of course, as they had to, as they wanted to. Letting him lead them anywhere he wanted to go.

I watched him lead the rats away, drawing my curled fingers along the length of the instrument, listening to her rustle in the grass behind me. I paid her no mind, just began wrapping my flute up, nesting inside the soft fabric.

"Mister," she said, from far off, still on the edge of shadow and light.

"Mister," she said again, and this time, she came closer still, squatting in front of me, the hem of her dress whispering against the grass. She touched my arm and I looked up at her, looked at her squarely for the first time. Her eyes, in the deepening dark, were a steely blue, almost purpled against the dusk. The mole at the side of her eye took on a shadow all its own.

We waited in silence, my hand falling still on the flute, only my thumb sliding over the very end of it, the sound a soft swash of skin and bone.

"I don't want to catch dirty old rats," she said, her nose wrinkled so that her mole bobbed against her eye. I felt a sudden, sharp catch in my chest that pushed my breath out in a near-laugh. Ah, girls. So hidden and yet so wanton in their desires. They always surprise you.

"What do you want to catch?" I asked.

She fell silent. She wasn't used to be asked about her wants; I could see it in her face as she considered this new thing, tongue flickering along her thumbnail. She shifted her eyes to the place where her brother had disappeared, and back to me.

Then she leaned in and whispered her soft girl-voice in my ear.

A stir of pride rose through me at her request, so strong it nearly knocked my breath out. Me – someone whose every breath mattered, whose every exhale made a note, a sound, a sound.

"Let's begin," I said when I could catch the air to speak again.

She'd learned a great deal listening to me teach her brother, just as I'd hoped she would. I made her create a rat flute just for practice, and her movements were quick and sure. She never hesitated or questioned. Merely moved the knife as though she'd done such a thing a hundred, a thousand times before.

"Now you can play it," I said when it was done.

But she only shook her head and tucked the tiny flute into her pocket, as though she knew it would do her no good to charm rats. As though she wasn't willing to waste the breath.

Her brother was back by then anyway, playing the creatures as a puppeteer plays his puppets. Forcing them to follow and back. He wasn't a master of creating his instrument, but it was clear he was learning how to control it and play it, as well as the creatures who followed.

"Now?" she asked.

I shook my head. "Another night." I wanted her to be sure. She was so young, after all.

———•◆•———

"Will it hurt him?" she asked.

"It will," I said.

But that didn't stop her.

"I'll make it quick," she said.

And she did.

———•◆•———

She learned to play her bone flute so well. Better than I ever did. Better than I ever will.

Her instrument is beautifully made, bearing five holes down the long, pink-hued bone. She inlaid the end with a few pieces of tooth, their off-white gleam shining as she moved. She played to the children in the cemetery, and of course they came to her, swirling and playing, curiosity glazing their eyes. The space was filled with the noise of children, and parents were happy for it, thinking them safe. Thinking them unspoiled between the graves of their loves ones, unmarked by the music that swelled and wheeled around them.

———•◆•———

What can I do now?" She'd taken to sitting on my lap while she played. I didn't mind. She had become in my mind, if not daughter, then student, protégé. I had grown both fond and proud of her. She was ever-curious, ever-learning. Writing new songs that made the children do things – tear the wings from butter-flies, snarl like wild dogs, hold hands and disappear off into the forest without a thought. Children were the hardest to enthrall, and yet they would do any-thing for her. They practically begged.

"What do you want to do?" I said. My hands traced her dress as it lay flared over my thighs, but I was thinking nothing of the action. I was thinking it was time to move on. To leave her to her studies, to see what she would do on her own. I was itching for a new student. My fingers ached to play again, to tame something new and wild. I missed that movement, that movement of first note, of first rapture. The pa-tience of waiting. She had surpassed me, and there was nothing more for me to do here.

"Watch," she said. She lifted the instrument to her lips, a few soft notes. A boy stepped forward, a girl too. They were watching her, their hands en-twined. That was her new song, making them touch. Hands. Fingers. Hips.

She played, and the children turned, mouths pressing together, such soft, tiny mouths. Perfect rosebuds. She played and their small bodies moved together, removed the air between them.

"Stop!" I had to push her off my lap so hard that her music flared and then faltered.

"But..." She pushed her lip out, near tears. Her mole slid, as though it was melting against her skin.

I took a softer tone. I didn't mean to scare her. I didn't mean to scare myself.

"You can't make people do those things," I said. "There is a line, a line of... " Of what? I didn't know.

She bit over her lip, nodding. I could not see her

eyes, and I knew there was something in there. Something I should have been wary of.

"Do you understand?" I asked, even though I wasn't sure I did.

She was still nodding. Chin up and down. The flute tucked behind her back like a secret.

"Good." I kneeled before her, looking up into that blue gaze, the pale lashes, the mole that perfected her beauty.

"I have to go away for a while," I said.

She would not meet my eyes.

The new flute is beautiful. More so than the last. Even I have to admit it. She made it all by herself, without any help from me. Seven holes, not five. Long and pinkish, starting to be worn smooth by her constant playing. A startling green gem, as if from a man's ring, inlaid at the end.

Leaning against the tree at night, her fingers fly, fly over the holes. Her music swells through the cemetery, between the graves, slides along the shadows and deepens them.

She makes me do things. Things I would never do. Things I should never do, not to a child, so soft, so pale, so perfect. But I cannot help it. She plays me, and I am hers.

SEED

CLARK HAS COME WITH HIS CHERRIES AGAIN. Carrying them in his ungloved hands, their skins touching his skin.

I take them delicately and without flinching, as I have been taught, my bare palms cupped for his offering, his dark red fruits tumbling into my hands. They are too much, too visceral, their blooded curves beckoning my tongue in a way that is not for polite company. Not even polite, paid company.

"Thank you, Clark," I say, now that his cherries are in my hands, and I can look away from them, to his face. He likes it when we address him by first name. Proper address – last, home, first – make his ruddy cheeks go more red and plump, like his cherries. Smind Kaja Meira says this means he is embarrassed or angered. So we must never call him Tupelo Oklahawma Clark, only ever Clark, and we must let him dump his cherries into the bowl of our cupped hands until they overflow, and if we can help it, we must not show our own embarrassment at their round, sweet scent against our noses.

"My pleasure, Sallie Kaja Arana," he says. The words come off his tongue slow and careful, and I know he has worked hard to memorize my whole name, even if he doesn't have the accents right.

"Just Arana," I say. "If it pleases you."

"It does," he says. And then like always, as if he's tasting my name in his mouth, a sound that makes me shiver and flush. "Arana."

I think he is a pretty man, although I don't know if that's true by his own people's standards. Big-bellied in a way that signifies his fecundity. Pale, barely pinkened skin that shows he spends much time in the common spaces. He wears many layers, his outfit cuts across him in funny places, belts at waist and ankle – but all of that serves to show more of his girth and weight, and perhaps that is the purpose. Still, I like him best of all when he is naked as the rest of us, just his skin and body, no artifices between us.

"Please make yourself at home," I say. Clark is already doing just that, but it's important to follow decorum, to say the things that we wish for our clients. Even the ones who pay with such high, personal prices as bright red cherries for something we should gladly give away for free. Smind Kaja Meira says this is the way of things, that one person's food is another person's lying with, and we should take what he offers and be grateful.

I prefer it, truly, to our own men, the skinny, boney ones who pay us in monies so that they may eat with us, so they may enter our private kitchenette spaces and feed us our own bits of day-old meat and scavenged berries. The way they watch my mouth chew and swallow, commanding me at their bidding. "Open your mouth," they say. "Let me see your tongue, your teeth. I want to watch you bite this. Now this. Swallow, oh the gods, swallow. Yes." Their bare hands touching my lips, their fingers tasting the secret inner places of my mouth. In exchange for this great and private thing, our own men try to shill us, to never pay in foods but always in the small, plain monies of the worlds, hardly worth a loaf of bread, a piece of dead fish.

Last year, one of the men took advantage of Gardin Kaja Kalliara while in her kitchenette, stuffing her mouth with quail bread until she could take no more, holding her against the table and force-feeding her from his own mouth, pieces chewed by his own teeth even after she'd said no and no again. We girls of Kaja's house do many things in our kitchenettes, things that would embarrass our great mothers if they knew, but to be forced, to eat from the mouth of another? No. Never. Smind Kaja Meira threw the man out, but it was too late. Gardin Kaja Kalliara had eaten her last meal at the hands of a gluttonist, a gorgist, the worst kind of rapist. We mourned her as we should a sister – returning each to our private kitchenettes the hour after her death, grieving for four days and four nights, putting out half our foodstuffs to share with her in a final breadbreak before she left for the aboveworld. But she never came to eat.

I don't care what the dissenters say; Smind Kaja Meira is right to advertise the House of Kaja to the men of Clark's kind, who pay us with what matters to share something freely given. Even if it embarrasses me so that I flush and blush and stammer.

"Make yourself comfortable," I say again to Clark, and there is something soft in my voice, because I mean it all the more after having thought of our own men, and what they want from me, from all of us.

"I will," Clark says. "Thank you."

It is odd to be standing here, just me and Clark in the common space. Usually there are many of us, but food has been scarce of late, and the other girls are out picking berries from the bottom of the hollow or scavenging scraps of meat from the leavings of yesterday's lion-killers.

"The other girls will be here soon." I try to keep the bowl of my hands still, so the cherries don't shift and draw attention to themselves.

"I don't care about the other girls, Arana." Clark has eyes of a color I've never seen before – only once in an elaborately wrapped piece of candy that tasted of mint leaves and winter breath – and each time he looks at me with his pale blue gaze, I don't know where to put my mind.

"I'll just take these to my quarters," I say, lifting the cherries closer to my mouth. So close that I can smell them, their pungent sweetness. The odor makes my mouth water, makes my stomach constrict with want. I cannot control it, and my head ducks slightly, until my lips nearly brush the fruits.

Clark barely notices, begins to untie his shoes, but I realize what I've done. "Forgive me," I say, my own voice choked. "Forgive me."

He looks up, his head cocked to the side, uncertain, his fingers stilled on their laces. "Arana?" he says. It is all question, one that I cannot answer.

It isn't polite to leave Clark there by himself,

without responding, but I have no choice. I can't believe I've done such a thing, brought food to my mouth in the presence of a semi-stranger, a client, an other, in the public place of the great room. The cherries are making me crazy, singing their scent-song to my mouth and belly.

I scurry toward the privacy of my kitchenette, the one place that is mine and mine alone in this whole big house of common rooms, dropping a few cherries along the way, but I don't bend to pick them up. I tell myself I will come back later, properly gloved, and pluck them from the hallway.

I shut the kitchenette door, leaning against it, my breath short and quick. The cherries roll from my fingers into the washbasin. I run cool water over them and over my wrists. I let my forehead drop to the side of the sink and get another whiff of the cherries, their pungent ripe perfume.

Clark is waiting for me back in the common room, probably beginning the slow take-off of his clothing, the way he does, folding the pieces carefully off to the side. I should not eat these cherries, not even one. I should not lick them the way that I am doing, should not be sinking my teeth into this one's stretched skin, letting its insides enter my mouth, fresh and sweet. But I cannot help it. It is done, and the thing is on my tongue and I am chewing and chewing and swallowing.

My body swells and puffs, myblood rises sugared and sweet inside me, surging into the heat of my cheeks and the pit of my belly. I try to keep the pleasure down, to not let it take over me, but it is hard and I cry out, soft, a mew that echoes around the basin. My hands tighten on the basin, hold on hard while my breath sinks and swims, sinks and swims, and I spit the stone from my teeth into the basin with a clatter.

Clark, I think. Clark has paid me in cherries and now I must leave them here, these beautiful round secret things and I must go and lie with him in the common space. I like to lie with him, as I like to lie with any who come – this is the secret of us, the one we hide so that we can eat. But the cherries. I think I like the cherries, the private place of them breaking open in my teeth, I like that best of all.

"Was that good for you, Arana?" Clark asks after and I nod. It is funny how they ask that, men of Clark's kind. Lying with is always good, always pleasurable, for us.

Usually, I like this part too, the after, resting among the pillows and the bodies, feeling everyone return to normal. But today it is, has remained, just the two of us. Something that has never happened before. Lying with is something you do with community, in the community places. But the girls have not come back, and it is just Clark and I here, our breaths quiet, his question breaking the stillness.

He takes my hand in his, and I twine my fingers to his in return. Our hands, our way of touching, this is all we are, this is what we do. Smind Kaja Meira says that other cultures eat together the way we lie with, that they gather in common rooms and feed in front of one another, gorging orgies of food and drink. I would not believe her, but it is Smind Kaja Meira, and she does not lie.

Smind Kaja Meira works hard to prepare us for our clients. First, she chooses us carefully, from the time we are old enough to eat alone, and then we are trained in many things: food care and preparation, together-eating, lips and tongue and swallow skills. Most of us also receive additional trainings: medical, cultural, historical, languages, hunting, defense. I am good with heavy pans and small kitchen knives – sometimes men come to me, not to eat, but to have me throw small, sharp blades into cutting boards they hold in front of their chests, and I never miss – but I have not been trained in culture. Smind Kaja Meira says I do not have the mind for it, and she is probably right. Still, I wonder sometimes, if all she says she knows is true, or if she sometimes makes it up, to help us attempt to understand the worlds.

Clark's flat palm runs up and down my side.

"Why do you never eat what I bring you?" Clark asks. "You always run off with it. Do you not like it?"

Where is Smind Kaja Meira? She should be here to answer questions like these. That is why she is house mistress here at Kaja – her smooth talk, her understanding of what men of Clark's kind really want to hear when they ask things like this. The sun slants sideways through the open spaces, and I think how she should be back by now, how all the girls should be back by now, and I feel the first stirrings of concern in my belly.

I smile at Clark, as I've been taught. Smind Kaja Meira says men of his kind like to know they're good at lying with, just as men of our kind like to know they're good at eating with, the private things we do in our kitchenettes.

"I like it very much," I say. And I mean both the

lying with and the cherries.

He smiles back, his face pretty pink like heated salmon, his teeth shimmery as scales. It would not do to admit that I have the desire to lick them. We do not touch mouths during lying with, not ever.

"Then we could do this again," he says. "Without the others?"

Our bodies are melded together, sticky from heat and grunt.

"Many girls, many pleasures is what Kaja offers," I say. "I am sorry my sisters are not here for you today." This is the other thing about Clark's kind of men – they want all of us at once, the more the better. That, Smind Kaja Meira says, is why they like us, why they pay us so well. Because we lie with in groups. She didn't say so, but she gave the impression that Clark's kind always lies with one-on-one or alone. I would like to ask him if this is true, but I do not think it is my place.

Clark rolls me over, so that I'm above him, my hands on his big, doughy belly. He is fuzzy like an animal there, in his upside-down bowl of soft flesh. "The other girls are nice, but I only care for you, Arana," he says. "I only want you."

There are his eyes beneath me, looking up into mine, mint and breath. He reaches up and touches my lip. Just for a moment. And I let him. Just for a moment.

This thing I am feeling does not have words. Not any words that I know of. I do not care to lie with him alone on purpose – I miss the mix and roll of the other girls, of watching their bodies move about Clark and myself – but his fingers are touching the gate to my most private of places, they are softly splitting it, and I am letting him.

The image that comes next is unbidden, shameful. Leading Clark alone, unpaid, back to my kitchenette, opening my mouth to his fingers lifting a cherry, taking the fruit between my teeth. The fruit and his fingers, my teeth and tongue. Showing him the insides of me. I want to hold a cherry up to his mouth, watch his lips open around it, see the skin split and spill fruit onto his tongue. Taste the food as it mingles with his breath.

"Arana?" he says. He shifts beneath me and I pull my mouth from his touch.

"I'm sorry, Clark. That is not possible." I can see from his face, the way it pinkens again, that he thinks I am talking about lying with, but I am talking about this thing I see, this desire that makes my mouth water so much it is hard to taste the words around it.

He starts to say something, but the door to the house opens to a whirr of girls and voices, Smind Kaja Meira's oddly loud among them.

"Careful with her," she says. And there, being laid on the golden pillows, is Alphie Kaja Therese, her pale skin scored with red stripes as though lion-marked, her long blonde curls filled with blood. She is young among us, with a laugh like copper bells, but is one of Smind Kaja Meira's favored. I cannot see her face, but I can hear her, small mews of pain and fear rising from her. The girls with care-training begin to tend to her, quick and efficient. The others stay back out of the way or scurry down the hallway toward their private spaces.

"What happened?" This is what Clark and I ask at the same time, and in voicing it, it somehow brings us closer together, not in a touching way, but in something else.

Ever the mistress, Smind Kaja Meira slides her gaze to us and her face takes on a calm smoothness. She puts her hands together, back-to-back, in a signal of benediction.

"I am sorry for the disturbance, Clark," she says. "Please forgive me, but one of our girls is injured and we must close the house. Only for a day or two, at most."

He rises with a big push, his weight lifting and leaving a blank space beside me. "I understand," he says. "What can I do?"

There is a brief moment of silence while Smind Kaja Meira considers his offer. She seems about to say something, and then says only, "Nothing, yet. But perhaps in the future. I am grateful for your offer. Now you must go."

I don't see him leave. I am standing and coming around to Alphie Kaja Therese, to the side of her. I am staring at her face, at the blood that cuts her skin into pale bits, the teeth that show, pinkened and exposed, where her lips should be.

"Who has done this, Smind Kaja Meira?" This is the question we all want an answer to. But for once, the mistress of our house has no answers. Or if she has them, she does not give them to us. We talk rumors about the lack of foodstuffs as of late, the wrath of neighboring houses who dislike Smind Kaja Meira's focus on men of Clark's kind. Some talk rumors about men of Clark's kind, but I do not join in those. Clark's kind of men are confusing, but I don't think they'd do such a thing.

"I know who has done this," says Zeern Kaja Steph. She is a small thing, bird-boned with dark hair and black eyes. She is culture-trained and often tells us tales from her classes with Smind Kaja Meira.

"Who?" we say. "Who?"

She lowers her voice. "Our own men. It is our own men."

"No," we say, and "No," again. But once she says that, as soon as her mouth opens and she puts the words into the world, she cannot take them back. And I cannot stop thinking of them.

The house is still closed, and for this I am glad. I do not want to take our own men back into my kitchenette. I don't want to eat – alone or in private. I don't even want to see Clark, his sweet-bowled belly, his mint eyes.

We are all busy doing what we can. With the doors closed for business, there is little money or foodstuffs crossing our threshold, and so the food-skilled must go gathering for all of us now, a job that is both coveted and feared. They go in groups of three, two for finding foodstuffs, one for protection. There have been no other attacks, but the girls who are foodseers say there is something metallic in the water, something bitter in the late summer grayberries that portends danger on the horizon, and so we are ever watchful.

I am one of the ones who guards the house now, patrolling the common spaces with my small, sharp knives held carefully in my fist, or standing at the door, asking who goes there and what their business is.

The healer-trained care for Alphie Kaja Therese day and night, washing the new blood from her face and hair, slathering her with poultices and herbs and bandages. She refuses to eat, shamed that she must be hand-fed by one of the other girls, right in the middle of the common room, for all to see. We have drawn cloths up around her face to give her some semblance of privacy, but still she says no. To force her would be against all we are, and yet if she does not eat, she will die.

Smind Kaja Meira sends me to beg of her to eat. The others have already done so, others with more power of persuasion, more skills in communication. I do not know what I can do that the others cannot. Still, I am made for duty. And so I slide under the white cloths that surround her, sit at her side. I cannot look into her face, the empty space where her lips should be, the way her teeth and gums show through the gap of her mouth. I cannot look at her at all, lest my stomach roll and give way, and for a long time I am shamed into silence by my own selfishness.

"Please, Alphie Kaja Therese," I say. "You must eat or you will not live."

Her words back are slurred and half-formed. Her tongue, too, was cut. Not from her mouth, but enough so I can hear her testing it, trying out its new shape as she speaks. "Like this?" she says. "Like this?"

"I don't know what you mean." Even though I do. How could I not? She could live, yes, but every day with her private places exposed for all to see. Men of our kind will watch her from the corners of their eyes and mouth-call, children will pantomime a drooling, gaping maw, women will say nothing but will turn their eyes away, in fear and in secret shame that they are suddenly glad again for their full lips, their closed mouths. She will be out of a job, out of a house. She will become two-named.

"Sallie Kaja Arana," she says, and she says it slow and careful, in a way that reminds me of Clark, and I suddenly miss his cherries, pouring from his skin into mine. "Look at me."

I look. It is all I can do. Her golden eyes close so that I can't look into them anymore, and my gaze moves down, toward that gaping place of her mouth. I am violating her even by my looking, and yet she has asked me to, and I must honor her request. A dozen teeth I can see, through the wide gap of healing skin. Her pale pink gums, the way they make half-moons around her teeth to hold them in. The red of her tongue as she speaks.

"Please." She takes me by the wrist, pushes her thumb into my veins with a sharp exhale of breath. My hand falls open, revealing the set of small knives there. "Please," she says. Her eyes open like golden apples, a sweet shine.

"No," I say.

She thinks I mean no to what she is asking. But that is not what I mean.

"Not with knives," I say. "Not with those." Knives are for throwing at men. Men who pay, and who hold cutting boards in front of their vital spaces as game. Men who don't pay and take lips and mouths that are not theirs as sport. Knives, these simple, sharp tools, these are not for Kaja's girls. These are not for us.

I ask the forbidden question: "What are your favorite foodstuffs?"

Silence and silence. I have overstepped, and I feel the pain for it, knives without knives threading my pulse.

Alphie Kaja Therese keeps hold of my wrist for a long time without saying anything. When she pulls me toward her, I lean in, my ear against her exposed places, as she whispers her list.

———————•◆•———————

I have no way to get a hold of Clark, and so I must find the foodstuffs on my own, the herbs too. I go out alone, against all rules, because what Alphie Kaja Therese asks is both private and forbidden. I carry my knives in my fist and my heart in my mouth, and I gather what is needed. I occasionally see groups of girls – two and one, scrounging and gathering – but they are easy to avoid. I see men of our own kind, too, alone mostly. I expect to be scared of them, or angered about Alphie Kaja Therese. But my knives stay in my palms and I find I am mostly tired from what I am about to do.

Alphie Kaja Therese deserves a feast, a private thing she makes alone and eats alone, in the privacy of her kitchenette. Instead, I gather what little of her list I am able to find. Tomatoes bought off a pathside vendor for the last of my monies, dug asparagus sprouts, mushrooms from beneath the moonwise tree. The herbs must be bought, and I have nothing but Clark's remaining cherries to trade. I take them – gloved, as I should – to the apothek, and hope she will give me two things in return: the herbs I need and silence. In the end, she does, but there is the understanding that I am still in her debt. I have promised her the next food to come into my hands from Clark, whatever it might be. Of course, I have not seen him since that night, so I can only hope he will return, that he has not found another house to take him in.

I prepare the food carefully, small container and gentle movements, and carry it to Alphie Kaja Therese in the midst of day, when most are out gathering and patrolling. I slip beneath the cloths and sit at her side. She is sitting up, reading from a book of philosophies, which surprises me for some reason. Perhaps it is because she looks so healthy and well, except for the red wound that dominates her face.

"Sallie Kaja Arana," she says. And although her lips are healing and her tongue is healing, she still says my name funny and I still cannot look at her mouth. "Where have you been?"

"I'm sorry I took so long," I say.

"I've just missed you," she says.

"I brought what you asked." I put the food container on the cushion next to her. "I will go, so you can partake in privacy, as you should."

She puts her hand, a pale fluttery thing, to my wrist. "I cannot," she says. "Smind Kaja Meira says I am to be found a home in Kyotti. I shall be Alphie Kyotti Therese."

"Kyotti? The call house?" A shudder ripples through me. I want to suppress it, that and the sound of my voice, but both come through, rise out of me. Smind Kaja Meira has told us of this place, where girls dance, their lips held open with metal bars and bits of wire. Where the two-mouthed open, gaping and aching, in time to music. I did not believe Smind Kaja Meira, but now I know it must be true. "No."

"Oh, yes. Smind Kaja Meira says she has lined it up." Her speech is much faster now, truer. "I shall lie on a pillow all day and they will pay to see my mouth, even as I sit. And I shall have my own kitch-enette and no one shall ever make me feed them again." Her voice has taken on a far-away sound, low and oddly off-key, and she isn't looking at me.

"Alphie Kaja Therese, you can't." Even as I say it, I know she can. She asked for death, and I have given her the chance to make that happen. Now she has asked for a second life, and Smind Kaja Meira has given her the chance to make that happen.

"Please do not tell Smind Kaja Meira," she says. "I did not tell her I asked for a last meal."

I nod – it is as much promise as my mouth will allow – and take the food away with me, dumping it into the waste of my kitchenette. The red-green juice of tomatoes and herbs, the fresh, dead scent of it as it drains away.

———•◆•———

I am not the one who finds Alphie Kaja Therese, and I am ashamed of how glad I am of that. It is one of the other girls, scavenging, who comes upon her, face-up, floating along the moonstream. Cut with a hundred knives. Or by a hundred men. Or by one knife and a hundred cuts.

"It is our men," say the girls. Or they say other things. That it was Clark's kind of men. That she had taken her own life. I throw my knives against the walls of my kitchenette. Again. Again. Until my hands tingle and my tongue is dried to the insides of my mouth.

Smind Kaja Meira calls me to her private kitch-enette. I have never been before, and I wait outside, unsure whether to knock or stand silent. Finally, she comes to the door on her own, as if she had known I was there.

"Come in," she says.

Her space smells of herbs and mushrooms and a clean that I cannot name. I avert my eyes from her private things, the utensils and fruits, and keep watch on my own belly, the pale skin of it bowing in and out as I listen. Even so, from the corner of my eye, I see her own knives glitter, sharp and silent, as she peels the soft golden skin from a hand-held pear, a hundred small, sharp cuts.

"I am sorry for our loss," I say, just to say something.

"As am I." Smind Kaja Meira stands, leaning her hip to her counter. Her movements are casual, at ease, as though she is alone here and unashamed. "But I have need of you now. Will you take Alphie Kaja Therese's place in the ranks?"

It is a question, but not a question at all. There is no need for me to even answer, beyond a formality, or to ask what that entails. I am for serving, and until she says otherwise, I am for serving Smind Kaja Meira. There is no other way to be.

"Of course," I say.

"You will find her murderer – it is our own men, I swear of it – and you will cut their lips out. Yes?"

Again, there is only one answer for a question from Smind Kaja Meira. Besides, it is what I want to do anyway. What my knives are for. Cutting. And revenge.

"Yes."

"And you will not speak of that again," she says. "No one is to know your role."

And no one does, not even as I track down the

men who say they did not kill our sister, even as I take their lips and tongue so they may not plead their false innocence again.

———◆——

As soon as the house re-opens, Clark returns. He is one of the first. I am on door duty, and so it is easy to see him. He wears his usual attire, although the belt cuts less deeply and his top hangs over him with more movement, as though he is less able to fill it than he was once. Two peaches nestle in his big palm. Their soft curves make my mouth ache and water.

In normal times, we would all be in our kitchenettes, making half of our food for Alphie Kaja Therese, helping her trip to the aboveworld. But these are not normal times. We are reopening, and I do not know if I am glad or anguished to see Clark standing at the door.

"Who goes there and what is your business with the House of Kaja?" I ask through the door, even though I can see it is him, Clark, the man I once thought of feeding from my own mouth. The very thought of it makes my cheeks heat with shame and want.

"I'm Clark," he says. "Don't you know me?"

His forehead wrinkles into waves and I don't need Smind Kaja Meira or anyone to tell me this means he has been made sad by what I have said. His face rises to mine, that mint-candy gaze, and I don't know where to put my stomach, this quieting in my belly.

"I know you," I say.

His face changes and pinkens, his lips open in a soft smile that shows me his shiny teeth. Then it slips away, into the opposite shape.

"I heard about your... " He stumbles over the word. " ...Sister. I'm sorry. She deserved better."

"She did."

We are quiet a long time, he on one side of the door with his peaches, I on the other side of the door with my knives.

"I brought you something," Clark says. "You don't have to be with me. You can have it."

He holds the fruit out, and when he smiles, he smiles big and full so that I can see his teeth. This is what Smind Kaja Meira wants for us. Men of Clark's kind and not men of our own.

I step outside the door, my feet on the outside ground for the first time in weeks. The gate shuts behind me with a clang.

Clark offers me one of his peaches, and I take it, skin on skin on skin, his hand to my hand. It is heavy and fuzzed, like the curve of his belly. With my knife, I cut a slice clean from the peach, and I think of skin falling open. I think of lips cut away, and I think of the work my hands will do, have done.

The juice runs down my wrist, to the elbow. A sticky trail.

There is no circus, I think, and I don't know where that thought came from. I do not like it, I do not want it, but now it is out, and I cannot take it back or let it go. It may have been our men who maimed Alphie Kaja Therese, but I know it was not our men who killed her. I think of Smind Kaja Meira's convictions, of her small paring knife and its perfect skin-slice. I think of my promise, how I am to cut the lips from those who killed my sister. I think I will find pleasure in it.

But first, there is Clark and his peaches.

"Eat with me," I say.

Clark dips his head at my request. He knows no hesitation. He knows not what I ask. And yet, he bows his head, the back of his neck pale and soft. His lips brush the sticky sweet skins of fruit and of me, and then he takes the soft peels of us into his mouth.

SEEING STARS

THE CALL COMES IN MID-SHIFT. As soon as I hear the address, I know who it is. Larson. A quick image of his face: skin pale as dry clouds, turquoise wing tats above both eyebrows. Irises dyed black to match his pupils. The way his eyes roll back when he's close to flying. He's been calling a lot lately.

I touch Bocco's shoulder. He pulls the mic out of his earlobe. I can't see his eyes through his vidshades, but I can tell by his raised eyebrows that he wasn't paying attention to the call.

"Frequent flyer," I say. "Larson."

Bocco nods, puts the rig in gear.

"Bagger, right?" he says. "Likes it long and slow?"

Bocco's never been great with names, but he can remember a gasper's meds and asphyx of choice for years. So I'm surprised when he gets this one wrong.

I flip on my medcom, talk into it before I answer. "Rig 014, clearing. ETA twelve minutes." When I click the medcom off, turn to Bocco. "No, he's a roper. Remember, blond guy?"

Bocco shakes his head. "Yeah, I know. He bagged last time. I took the call with, uh," Bocco snaps his fingers. "The newbie, Dennie."

"Shit," I say. "He bagged? Seriously?" Bagging's a slippery slope, one I don't like to see clients go down. Especially not clients like Larson. Maybe I can talk him into scarfing or roping instead. Something, anything else.

Bocco shrugs. As the pilot, he doesn't see the clients. Most calls, it's just me and the gasper, unless something goes wrong. And even then, it's just me and the client until backup arrives.

I look out the front window of the rig. The sky's as still and bright as always. No clouds, no rain. We haven't had real dark or real stars in so many years I can't remember.

Bocco raises the silent rig off the landpad. Below, the city is all high-rise and lights. The sky's been like day since I was a teen. It's not that the dark's not out there anymore—it is. It's just that we've got so many lights going all the time that you can't see it. So gradual, you almost didn't notice the night fading. When I was still little, my dad took me to this dark park. We lay on blankets and looked up. You could see dark, like a cellar that never ended. But the stars, that's what I loved. So many, so deep and complex. My dad pointed out constellations – the hunter, the dippers – but all I saw were worlds and worlds of light, shining down on me. I've never seen anything like it. I probably never will again.

I turn away from the view of the city, touch Bocco's cheek, right below where the vidshades sit. "Shades, Bocco."

He flips off his vidshades and pulls them from

his face. He likes to fly with them on, so he doesn't miss a minute of whatever whackball game he's watching, but it makes me nervous. After five years of running together, after five years of fucking each other, I've finally gotten him to the point where he'll drive without vidshades. Small accomplishments.

I settle in my seat as Bocco takes off. Truth is, with or without the vidshades, Bocco's a solid pilot, fast and smooth. Some of the guys pilot the rig like they're wagging their cock at the sun. Not Bocco. It was the first thing that turned me on about him when we met. Bocco fucks like he flies, slow and careful. No showoff, no tricks. Straight in and out. After spending my days with clients who need to die to get off, straight in and out is the only kind of sex I want.

Bocco will say I fell for him because he's the only guy around with a cock, and there is some truth to that. The cock stuff anyway. Unlike the male meds, male pilots don't have to be snipped. The meds are all Uneds, except me. But that's because I'm a female, so no worries about me falling under the asphyx spell. I'd guess most meds are former baggers themselves, but it's not my place to ask.

While Bocco flies, I swivel my seat so I'm facing the back. The console center looks like those spaceships you used to see in movies, before we built enough spaceships to know what they really looked like. My guess is somebody at AEA copied the old Hal movie when they designed this – about a million buttons and lights, most of which do nothing. Talk about life imitating art.

I punch the buttons that will mix up Larson's doses, and then let the machine do its work. Protocol forbids doing this ahead of time; tells me to wait and see if I can't talk him out of it, just this once. Send him away with a bit of porn and a smile. But that's always seemed out of step with what we're really doing here. Safe play is only safe play in the hands of a professional. At least, that's the corporate line.

My Hal computer beeps. The computer had delivered Larson's dosage in three tiny syringes that self-stick to my fingertips. The first is the big deal – the one that enhances his dying orgasm. The second gives his blood three seconds' worth of vital oxygen. The third – well, the third I've never had to use.

I stick the syringes to the fingers of my left hand, leaving my thumb and forefinger free. Then I flex my fingers, making sure the syringes are hidden. The illusion must be perfect.

Bocco gets us there in record time, mostly keeping quiet. Only a tight-lipped "This guy ought to have his own landing pad" as he sets the rig down softly on the roof of Larson's condo. We're a blank rig, meaning we don't advertise what we do, but I'm sure everyone knows it, just by virtue of it being blank. The equivalent of those packages that used to be shipped in a plain brown wrapper.

"Nice land," I say.

"Soft as a baby's ass," Bocco says. Which makes us both laugh. Neither of us knows what a baby's ass feels like. I pinch my fingers around Bocco's earlobe, just for a second, and give a tug. He grins, and pats my thigh.

I pick up my jump kit. It's designed to look like a large purse or a shopping bag, depending. The top compartment is filled with ropes, plastic bags, a few disposable toys, porn. The hidden compartment, opened by my voice, is where I keep the stuff that matters: safe-meds, verbal insurance policy, subcute tape. I've never used anything in the kit – most clients have their own supply of equipment, and I'm careful, so I don't have to open the hidden compartment. Still, I'm superstitious – I take it with me because I know that the first time I leave it behind will be the first time I need it.

I hop out of the rig, smooth my jumpsuit down. They're new this year, a kind of fabric that bends the light to make the eye tired, suggests that it move on to other, more interesting things. It helps create the illusion that our clients are alone when they come.

Bocco's got his vidshades back on, his mic in. I lean in, wiggle my needled hand at him.

"Give me twenty," I say. Then I remember Bocco saying *bagger*, saying *long and slow*, and change my mind. "No, more like thirty."

Bocco nods, although I have no idea if he's heard me. I slide the door shut behind me, take a deep breath, and pop the button on the elevator that will take me to Larson's place.

———◆◆◆———

The deal is that I'm supposed to just let myself in. It always feels a little odd, like I'm invading a client's space, even though they ask for us and pay for us to be here. I put my thumb against the key screen, and wait until the door clicks green before I push it open.

The place is stark, like so many of our clients'. Real world doesn't offer much anymore. Even before I get to Larson's gameroom, I can hear the holographs, all women from the sounds of it, panting in fast, shallow hisses. Used to be, people thought gaspers were either all gay or cross-dressers. Of course, that was mainly just what made the news. Easier to sell the story of a young man who's accidentally offed himself in a dress. My experience says Larson's pretty much the typical: male, white, career-driven, mostly hetero, and bored out of his skull.

When I enter the room, I see the holo women, three of them, tied in a tangle of arms and limbs and breasts. Every inch of skin, every movement and sigh impossibly perfect. But even that, I know, is not enough.

Larson is lying face down on his game table. He's naked, and looking away from me, watching the holo girls. A long thin rope hangs from the ceiling, the end a perfectly knotted noose, but it's dusty. And I don't see his usual assortment of scarves. So he is bagging then. For a second, I regret the needles already on my fingers. Maybe I can still talk him out of it.

But then he turns, looks over his shoulder at me. For the moment, he still sees me, even around the jumpsuit, around the expectation of pleasure. For the first time, his irises aren't dyed black. They're sky blue, so bright that his eyes look fake, except for the broken blood vessels through the whites. Since last time I saw him, he's had rows of white feathers added to the blue wing tats above his eyebrows.

He smiles. His teeth are perfectly white. "I was hoping it would be you."

I put my jump kit down next to the door, act like I didn't hear his comment. Meds walk a fine line. We're supposed to be as anonymous as sex workers, as comfortable as doctors. And clients definitely are not supposed to hope for one of us in particular. I make a mental note to mark myself off Larson's page when I get back to the rig.

Larson gestures at the wavering girls. "What do you think of my newbies?" he asks.

"They're lovely," I say.

I step up close to him. I could touch him from here, but touching is prohibited. Instead I take a visual physical: good muscle tone, not too thin. His breathing, at least for the moment, is regular. He has the kind of ass people pay for, round and muscular, but I think his is real. No scar marks. Snake hips, wide back. For a second, all I can think is, what a waste. How many people would kill just to get off with him. And here he is, thinking that he's paying me to kill him so he can get off.

I'm open-minded about what gets us off. But it's still hard to watch someone die under your supervision, just for pleasure. I think about what Bocco and I do, the way our fucking is almost subversive in its normality. Me on top, fingering myself until I come, and then we change places for Bocco's turn. Is the pleasure different somehow? Or does Larson just need more to truly get off?

It isn't my place to ask, so I stand at the head of the table, waiting. My job is one, to soft-sell something less dangerous if I can; two, to keep him alive; and three, to bring him back to life after if I can't. Holo girl, therapist, medic. I am all three.

Larson's back rises as he inhales. His voice is so low I barely hear him. "I almost didn't call today."

My breath catches in my throat. I force it out, inhale another before I speak. Even so, my voice sounds off. I hope he can't hear it above the girls' moans.

"You know you can call anytime," I say, the corporate line falling from my mouth with ease. "That's why we're here, to enhance your pleasure in a safe, secure way."

There's a truth to this, and a not-truth. AEA might have started as a goodwill organization – clean needles, free condoms, med-supervised asphyxiation – but that was way before my time. Now, we're a publicly traded company. Our clients are the high-end of the high-end. Our CEO's motto is, you pay to play. I tell myself that we're doing good every day, but I don't believe it. I don't let myself think about the guys who don't have apartments and jobs like Larson.

I put my hand over the muscles of his shoulder, let it hover an inch above his skin. He radiates a kind of jumped-up heat. It pulls on my needled fingers, makes the pulse beat hard in the tips of them.

"We could do something else?" I suggest. "We could watch the girls, masturbate together?" My voice sounds hollow, even to me. When I was still in med school, I worked at a fly-up take-out place. Hello, may I take your order, thanks, have a great day. The bosses were always on our asses to upsell, to add on. Want a side of crack-ups with that? How about an O_2 hit in your shake? I hated trying to talk people into something they didn't want. I feel like that now, trying to talk Larson into straight masturbation.

He rolls over, leans his head back on his hands. His cock is half-hard, coated in saliva or lube. He's jerked off once already, to get himself ready, to make this one last.

"That's sweet," he says. Those blue eyes seem like he means it. For a second, I believe it was that easy to talk him out of it. Then he clenches his fists, a quick open and release. "But let's do this. Everything's under the table."

I reach into the box beneath the table, hoping for hidden scarves, a rope. Instead, I find a clear bag, carefully folded. It's special-made, with thick fabric. The front is curved to fit closely over a face. A black pull-cord is sewn around the opening.

My hands shake around the bag, rattling the plastic. Scarfing, hanging, roping, there are so many ways. But bagging is the worst for me, watching the way their faces look beneath the plastic, sucking in, mouths and eyes open, like plastic-covered dolls.

I move into position at the top of Larson's head. He takes a deep inhale, shakes his hands out. He licks his palm, smearing it with saliva, then sucks on each of his fingers, wetting them. He wraps his fist around his cock, starts pumping the base with short motions. With his other hand, he pinches his nipple.

I hold the bag near his head, steady, ready. This, the before, is the part of this job I like, when clients are just masturbating, straight up, getting close. I feel lucky to get to see this part, before the end: how different people are in what they do, how every hand holds every cock a little differently, how every hand and every cock is different. Larson's moans are different too, low and guttural. His eyes are closed, lashes fluttering against his pale cheeks. The way his forehead tightens, it's like his wing tats are fluttering, trying to fly.

Watching him like this, my body responds. I tell myself that I'm not turned on, I'm just curious, just doing my job. That I want to hold him here, at this moment, when it seems all pleasure and no pain. But

I know that's not enough for him. It will never be enough for someone like Larson.

Larson opens his blue eyes. "Bag me," he says.

I slide the bag down over the top of his head. He lifts the back of his head, and I work the bag down to his neck, leaving the bottom open. It's tricky, breathing, not breathing, the illusion of death. Close the bag too soon, and he's really dead. Close it too late, and he doesn't get his fix, and then he tries again later, without me here to help. Either way, I know it's his life in my hands, this bag and rope. There's a power in this that scares the shit out of me. It also makes my body feel alive. I may talk the talk – love what I do, helping people – but in this moment, right here, when it's just me and the client on the table... I'm addicted to this moment as much as my clients are to their orgasmic deaths.

On the table, Larson moans, deep and low, drowning out the holo girls. He pumps with his fist, up and down, his cock fully hard now. His thin hips rise and fall on the table.

Watching, I let out a low soft moan of my own. Then I shake my head, force myself to look back at his face under the bag, to remind myself of what I'm doing here. I wish he would close his eyes. Usually, it doesn't matter – they're so black they're like nothings. But now, without the dye, they're right on me, blue, human. He's not supposed to be watching me. I put my arms up, hoping the jumpsuit will distract him, take his eyes somewhere else.

It doesn't work, so I look down at his body for telltale signs. His breathing is fast and tight, his cock leaking precum. He twists his nipple, hard, and gasps.

"Now. Now," he says.

I pull the bag closed at the same time I puncture his neck with the first of the needles. The needle is so small he wouldn't feel it even if all of his nerve endings weren't already centered in his cock. I know it goes in though, ups his pleasure, by the way he arches his back. His big toes curl down.

"Aw, God," he says. I think he's coming, so I hold the second needle over his shoulder. But Larson takes his hand off his nipple, reaches over his head and grabs my wrist. We've never touched before. His fingerpads are callused, his thumb strong. The heat I felt before is ten-fold, seeping into my skin.

"Join me," he says, his mouth making the plastic bag crinkle. His eyes are darker, deeper blue. They hold me in place. He's still working his cock, faster and faster. In this moment, as his body hovers between life and death, he is more alive than I've ever seen. His veins work their thin blue magic beneath the surface of his skin, bringing him the last of the oxygen. His hand works the thin length of his cock, bringing him the beginning of pleasure.

His hand on my wrist tightens. My own veins slow down. Every pulse is loud and slow. Every one takes seconds to start, to finish.

"Please," he mouths. "I want to show you…"

I pull my hand from his grasp, stumble back. I trip over my jump kit and nearly go down. I move back until I am out of reach of his hands. His voice is barely audible.

"…show you the stars," Larson says.

There is no air left. My own lungs hitch as the bag goes tight around Larson's face. The plastic makes a little cave in his mouth, as he sucks in, his body trying for one final breath. And then he's coming and dying all at once, his hand rigid around his cock, cum spraying the holo girls, his blue eyes rolling back in his head. His mouth works beneath the plastic, but there is no sound.

It takes one second too long before I can right myself, get back to Larson's body. The second needle, with its hit of oxygen, goes into his shoulder two seconds too late. Already his lips are tinged blue. His body hitches, shudders.

"Fuck, Larson." I try to rip the bag from his mouth, but it's expensive, well-made, and the fabric just stretches beneath my nails. Larson's eyes are rolling back down, he's coming down from the pleasure, and in about a second, all he's going to feel, if he's capable of feeling anything, is his body dying. I pull at the rope at the bag's opening, ranting. "Fuck this, this fucking job, fuck this, fuck this," but my words don't help get air into Larson's throat.

My fingers fumble with the rope. It's twisted itself into some kind of knot. I'm holding my breath. I can't let myself inhale until Larson does. Larson's body goes still on the table, his mouth and eyes open beneath the plastic. I want to pummel his chest, breathe into his mouth like I learned in med school.

There's a knife in the secret compartment of my kit. I'm about to get it when the knot loosens. I pull the rope and it comes untied. I slide the bag off Larson's warm, sweaty face as fast as I can, praying for a breath, a pulse, anything that would mean I don't have to use the third needle.

My fingers to his neck. Nothing. "Fuck!" It's a long, low moan of a word. And then I put the third needle against Larson's still artery. Even though I've never used it, I know what's it in: Fast-acting epi to start the heart, slow-acting sed to put him in a temporary coma while he recovers. From the death I gave him.

I inhale, hold my breath until I have the right angle of needle to vein. Then I press the needle into his shoulder. The response is instant: a gasp, a shudder. Larson looks right at me, at my face above the jumpsuit. "Did you see them?" he asks. "My god, the stars." And then the sed kicks in, and he sleeps.

———◆———

While he's out, I lean into my jump kit and say "Draco" to open the secret compartment. Inside is the fourth needle, the one that is neither legal nor acknowledged. It's a black market med designed for warfare. I don't ask how our company gets it, I'm just glad to have it. I pop the end and press it into Larson's neck vein. Filled with a mild amnesiac, something to forget us by. Clients may want to almost die to get off, but clients who actually die tend to be a little pissed. I can't imagine why.

So when Larson wakes, he thanks me. His words are slurred, but he doesn't seem to notice. "That was... amazing," he says from the bed. "Flying."

I've already scanned his vitals, his nons, while he was out, so I know he's going to be fine. Protocol says I have to stay until he wakes, but I can't wait to get out, I can't wait until he's not watching me with those blue eyes. My hands won't stop shaking. I think of Bocco waiting for me in the rig, calm and collected as always, plugged in, but it doesn't help.

"How do you feel?" I ask.

"Do you have to ask?" he says.

"Yes, I do," I say. "Protocol."

"The best," he says, drawing out the *st* like a sigh. Despite everything, because of everything, he has this grin. A big wide smile. His body is relaxed on the bed, all tension gone, everything emptied. Clean slate. As if to echo what I'm seeing, he says, "I'm reborn."

He reaches his hand above the bed. I know he's reaching to me, to the me he thinks I am. His hand is so close I can feel the heat, slow and steady, that's rolling off him.

"Sadie, thank you."

It startles me that he knows my name.

"Okay, then," I say. I step away from his outstretched hand, throw my jump kit over my shoulder. It's a sign that we're near the end of this call, a reminder to Larson that I have other clients to attend. While he was out, I stuffed his asphyx bag in my jump kit, hoping he won't miss it, although I know he will. The front of the plastic is all stretched where I tried to rip it to let him breathe. Now it crinkles when I move. I try to stand still, but his eyes are making me jumpy. Like there's too much oxygen in my lungs.

"You could, you know," he says. "I could show you."

I finger the strap of my bag. Inside the jumpsuit, my skin has grown hot, sticky.

"Show me what?" I ask.

"All of it: life, death, the world. Don't you, don't you want to know, don't you want to feel it?"

I tell myself that he's no different than a junkie, trying to turn me on to his drug of choice. No different.

But I clamp my hand to my side to keep from stepping forward, to keep from putting my hand inside his. It scares me, how badly I want to reach back, to feel those hands. How badly I want to see something new again, stars or death or whatever it is that would change me.

"No, no I don't." I take a step back. The plastic bag crinkles, loud, inside my jump kit. "If you're feeling okay, then I have to go." Without waiting for an answer, I step back through the empty white rooms.

———◆———

Outside, my hands shake so hard that I can barely get the rig door open. Bocco leans over the seat and helps me inside.

"What happened?" he asks. "That took forever. I almost came in there, but I didn't know."

He speaks in a rush. His vidshades are on the dash. He doesn't even have his mic in. I drop my bag on the floor and put my palm on his flushed cheek.

"I'm sorry," I say. "I just... it just took longer than expected."

Bocco turns my hand over, squints at the three used needles under my fingertips.

"Went bad on you, didn't it?"

My throat opens to speak. Instead, I give a choked sob. I press my face into the dark space beneath Bocco's chin.

His big hands rub the hollow between my shoulder blades.

"It's okay," he says.

It's not, but I want to believe it is; or at the very least, I want to not think about it, so I put my lips against the bottom of Bocco's chin. I kiss up until I'm at his lips. I keep kissing him, feeling the warmth of his mouth, the way he opens his lips with an exhale to let me in.

But after a second, he pulls back and puts his hand on the gear shift.

"Better?" he asks. "Want to call in?"

I shake my head. I'm not ready. My blood runs heavy in my veins. The sky is too bright against my eyes.

"Fuck me, Bocco," I say. My fingers tremble at the opening of my jumpsuit, the clasps that slide up both legs and end in the crotch. I pull, and the clasps come undone with small pops.

Even with the jumpsuit, Bocco's eyes don't get tired, don't move elsewhere.

Still he says, "Not here. We're working."

But I press myself to him. I know what I'm doing even as I do it, forcing his hand with my body. I put his hand on my bare leg, move out of my seat and into his.

"Yes, here," I say. "Please, quick."

I cover his mouth again with my lips so he can't say anything. He responds with his body, his hands and hips and hardening cock. Without breaking the kiss, I lift myself off his lap just enough to open the fly of his flight suit.

His cock is long and hard already in my hands. I wrap my hand around the thickness of it, but that reminds me too much of Larson, so I let go, lower myself down until Bocco's whole cock disappears inside me.

It's good. It helps. But even as we're fucking, even as Bocco is holding my hips, raising and lowering me over his cock, even as I'm shuddering over him, I know it's not enough anymore. It is too grounded. Too simple. Something has changed, something I want.

I can't say what it is, even as Bocco holds me after, rubs his big hands across my hair, tells me what he thinks are the right things, says he thinks he loves me. I close my eyes against the light as Bocco pilots us back to the base, and I try to pretend I am like I was, before.

It is only later, prepping my jump kit, that I find the crumpled-up asphyx bag, its heavy plastic front stretched but not broken. I realize that I never took my name off Larson's call list. I think about his hand held out to me, his offer. "I can show you the stars," he'd promised. And then he'd seen them. Somehow, in the gap between life and death, he had found the dark.

Now, I sit in the rig, watch the bright sky through the window. I don't say anything when Bocco drives with his vidshades on. Inside my jumpsuit, pressed close to my body, is a plastic bag. When I'm alone, I run my fingers over the stretched plastic, the silky black rope that draws it closed. And I wait. I wait for the call, the one that will bring the image of his face: his turquoise wing tats, his lips in a wide smile, his blue eyes open to his secret, starry dark.

ANIMAL INSTINCTS

THE FOAL IS STILLBORN. I hear the mother's grief long before we get the baby out of her. It is in the lowered stance of her head, the way her eyes stay half-closed, as if they can't be bothered to see, the soft sounds that are neither whinny nor groan but something in between.

My forehead rests against the mare's sweaty neck, my fingers threaded through her mane in a clench of sympathy. She leans hard against me. For the moment, I am her herd, and she is mine.

Daniel, the vet that takes care of high-end horses at race farms like this one, as well as most of the other large animals in the county, is tugging the dead body of the creature from her. The mare's pulse gallops through her tired, straining neck. There is the wet sound that the dead make when they slide from the living, and then it is over.

Daniel kneels over the dead creature in the straw, an unmoving bulk of black and white. Long dark legs with tiny, too-soft hooves. A white blaze like lightning down its face. White socks pulled half-way up on both hind legs.

"Shame," Daniel says. "Good blood. Would have made a great-looking filly."

From elsewhere inside the huge barn, something metal and loud clangs against cement, and the mare and I both jump. I tighten my fingers inside her mane, holding us both still against the noise.

Barely noticing the sound, Daniel stands, knees popping. "Mare's all yours, Mags," he says.

He reaches down for the foal. He would take her and do whatever it is vets do with the dead. Bury or dissect. I don't ask. I was in vet school myself once. It wasn't the studying or the tests that got me – although everyone predicted that an autistic, even a mild autistic such as myself, would never make it through those. It was the animals. The first time I was supposed to take the ovaries from a ewe, a living ewe, my ewe, the one I'd raised from a lamb and fed with a bottle in my second year, I knew that I was done.

"Leave the foal," I say against the mare's grey coat. My lips are coated with the salt of her sweat and pain. "The mare needs to grieve."

This is what I say. What I don't say is this: the soul bearer is still here. I can hear it, snorting around the foal, feet shuffling, big teeth chewing. I don't look up; I've seen them before, pig-headed with sharp white teeth. I've also seen what happens when you interrupt their feeding. The creature dips its head into the foal's belly, pulls something out with a slick sound. I shudder at the noise, and the mare echoes my movement, her ears flicking back.

Daniel shrugs, steps away without touching the

foal. I am pretty sure he likes me as a person. This is the kind of thing he would say – "I like her fine as a person" – but he doesn't have to, because I know it the same way I know that the mare's sighs of pain are not entirely physical. So Daniel might like me as a person – he calls me Mags, after all, not Maggie or Miss Munroe – but he doesn't like what I do. He doesn't believe in it. To him, animals are just animals. Instinctual creatures. Operating out of nothing more than pain, hunger, fear. "Waste of money." He'd say this too, about what I do. But he doesn't have to. I know how he feels.

He hesitates a moment. I can feel his gaze on the back of my neck, as though he's considering saying something else, then he steps away. The sounds of his footsteps across the straw are a dry comfort compared to the slick meaty noise of the creature behind me.

"See you around, Mags," Daniel says as he goes.

I lift my hand in a wave without pulling my forehead from the mare's quivering muscles and skin. His job here is over. Mine has just begun.

<hr />

"You want me to pick you up?" Joan asks. I've told her about the foal, but not the bearer. The visible world is hard enough for her. She asked about the foal, and I tried to keep the images short because she's told me they disturb her. But I went on too long, in too much detail, and now she wants to take action, to quiet me. Not in a bad way, I know.

"I don't mind," she adds when I don't say anything. Her voice is hiss and static on the cell phone. I flinch from the other noises, even as I press my ear to the sound of her voice.

I don't drive. It's a skill Joan has captured but I have not. She likes the rules, she says. They make her feel safe, like so many step-by-step procedures do. Me, on the other hand, the very thought of trying to understand and remember the rules of it makes me nervous. Sometimes listening to her recite them – key in, turn, shift into drive – forces my throat to close up. In my mind, I can see images of every accident I've ever run across; they flip through my brain like a picture book.

"No, I don't mind the walk," I say. "I can let go of the pictures in my brain."

"And all of the filth on your body too," she says.

"I'll shower before I come in."

"I know you will." Her voice is quiet. Kind of tired.

I remember what I meant to ask. "How are you? How is the baby?"

Her laugh, even through the phone, looks like her – blonde and curly-headed. Her rosy cheeks and rosy nipples. The soft curves of her hips and muscled legs. "I'm fine," she says. "The baby's kicking. Come home. I made quiet chicken and rice."

We aren't supposed to work, Joan and me. One highly functioning autistic who thinks in pictures and not emotions. One in-control obsessive-compulsive who needs rules for her rules. And we definitely aren't supposed to have children. But here we are. Here I am, showering away the day so that I don't screw up her order. Here she is, knowing that I can't bear the sound of chewing, so she makes soft rice and chicken without skin so that we can have dinner together.

"I'll be home as soon as I can," I say. My eyes close and I can see her in my head, the way she is when the OCD isn't bad and she can throw her arms around me without worrying about dirt and germs. She's gotten worse since the baby. Protective. Probably we both have.

"Don't forget to shower," she says, as if she knows what I'm thinking.

"I won't," I say. I mean it.

This is as close as we can come to talking about love, but we both know it's there. Just like we both know that our decision to have a baby, to have Joan carry it, was the right one. No matter what anyone says.

My work takes me all over the county. Mostly, I walk if I can. If I can't, I ride with one of the vets, like Daniel, or the farmers themselves. Today, it's a breeder sow, blue ribbon pig that won't load. They've tried it the nice way, and she's bitten two farm hands. They don't dare try it with ropes and winches – she's bred, and just barely, and they're afraid she'll lose the whole lot.

"Christ, she's huge." It's Daniel again – we seem to be running in the same work cycles at the moment.

Inside the sty, the sow flicks her ears. She's dirty pink, with massive jowls under her chin, snorting in the direction of our legs as we stand outside the sty. I am careful to keep the deaths from Joan, but also the dirt. If she saw this, the way I'm standing knee-deep in mud and pig shit and slop, so high it almost comes over my barn boots, she might never let me in the house again.

"Well, what'll we do?" The farmer is the kind of man you can tell only has an eye for his wallet. He spits and curses; he's just mad that pig is being bothersome, that she won't load. His gaze goes to Daniel, but he never looks at me. He might have hired me, but he doesn't want to admit it. Animals are just animals, after all.

The pig shuffles toward us, snuffling. The whiskers on her chin are stiff and coated in dirt. Her lips curl back and I see her teeth. Big and hard and yellow. Pointed at the ends. She lifts her head, eying me with dark, black eyes. Bottomless and empty.

I back up, my boots sticking in the mud so that I nearly fall backwards. Everything rushes at me – every bearer I've ever seen, every snorting nose and wide mouth. Every slickening sound of body parts between those sharp teeth.

Daniel puts a hand on my hip, as though to catch me, and I shake him away. My voice is shaking, but not so much that I can't speak. "Get a pail, deep," I say. The image of the kind of pail I want flickers in my brain. "A pickle pail. Some grain at the bottom."

The farmer brings it and holds it out to me. My hands reach, but I can't take it. I have to shake my head. "You'll want to make it safe," I say, "The pail over its head, lead it backwards. She won't be stressed."

The farmer spits again. "That's what I'm paying you for? So you can tell me what to do? You're not even going to get your ass in there and do it?"

"I'm sorry," I say. But I'm not. I'm afraid. This lying is something I've learned. It makes people's energy change, makes them calm. They can't read me like the animals can.

Daniel and the farmer do what I say, my words

guiding them from the sidelines. They offer her the grain at the bottom of the bucket, they talk soft to her. "Sooie," they whisper. "Sooie." The pig dips her head deep into the circle of the pail, eating the grain, comforted and fed. She loads up for the trip just fine.

I have to walk home, all five miles, just to wash the fear off.

———◆•◆•◆———

There's something Joan wants to tell me at dinner, but doesn't. I wait for her to say what it is. It's no use asking and I don't have the right words anyway. After dinner, she cleans in that ordered way that she has and I shower again. Almost always, we sleep in separate rooms – she can't bear the filth that falls from us when we sleep; I can't sleep with the noise of her breath – but usually we meet in her bed for a bit in the evenings.

"Joan?" I say it soft, my clean feet still on the bottom of the tub.

"Come into bed!" Joan yells from her bedroom. I am smiling even as I dry off. It makes me happy when she calls me like that, when I've been given permission to enter. It's like our love has conquered something unconquerable, if only for a little while.

I step from the shower, dry off, and then walk carefully across the towels she's laid down. Six steps from bathroom to bed, each of them centered squarely on the terry cloth squares.

From there, I can get into bed with her and she doesn't have to worry about germs or dirt. When I slide beneath the covers, she turns on her side, puts one hand on the side of my cheek. Her skin is cool, like outdoor water.

"Kiss me," she says. This is our ritual: she lets me know what she can handle by asking for it, and I comply. Her lips taste like soap and the mint of toothpaste and, beneath that, her mouth, the length of her tongue, tastes of butter, salty and rich.

While we're kissing, she takes my hand and puts it on her bare, round belly. Beneath the skin, the child, our child, ripples and wriggles. I laugh against her lips and then pull away, just to watch the movement beneath her skin.

"The baby likes that," I say.

"Yes," Joan says. "Me too. Do it again."

So I do, and I lean into her so that our bellies are together, and the baby's wiggling makes me laugh, like tickling.

"The doctor came today," Joan says when she has her mouth back. Our OGBYN comes to our house because Joan can't bear the hospital, all the germs, all the dirty tiles, all the sick people. It was one of the things we asked her before we got pregnant, if she would come and see Joan here, in her own bed.

I lean up on my elbow. "She did?"

Her blue eyes are shiny as she puts her hand over mine. "It's a girl," Joan says. "A girl. One more girl in our family."

"I knew that," I say. I did know that, somehow. I have pictured the baby a hundred times, with Joan's blonde curls and her blue eyes, in a pink and blue dress. Ten short fingers. Dimples when she smiles, and soft, small teeth, even though I know she won't have them yet.

"Of course you did," Joan says with a quiet laugh. My hand caught between hers looks like a skin sandwich; her pulse above and below. "Our little Seed."

I curve my palm around the bottom of her belly, imagining a tiny red seed inside her, growing bigger and bigger. "Our little Apple," I say.

"Macintosh?" she says. Her laugh is curls bouncing and wrinkles like love lines at the corners of her eyes.

"Mac's a boy's name," I say. We haven't talked about names before. We don't want to jinx anything. Not too early. Not getting our hopes up.

"Could be either," she says.

"True," I say. I slip my fingers down, let one play around the indent of her belly button, which is disappearing day by day as the baby, as our daughter, grows inside her. "How about Ida Red?" I say.

"Oh, yes," Joan says.

And Ida Red she is.

"Hello, Ida Red," I say with my hand on Joan's belly. I can see her already.

———◆◆———

"Mags?" It's Daniel, leaning over the stall where I'm sitting in the straw with a three-year-old thoroughbred that got attacked by a mountain lion. Her flanks are scraped with claw scars. If someone tries to touch her, she skits and rolls, panicking. I've been sitting in her stall all day, letting her get used to me. She's still in the corner, shivering. Daniel's voice makes her eyes roll to their whites and she half-turns, her hind feet aimed near my face.

My voice is low as I scramble sideways. "What are you doing here? She's going to freak."

"Mags, you should come out." His energy is all weird, ping-ponging worse than the mare's. I step out of the stall.

He says, "There's been an accident, with Joan."

He says a lot of other things, but I don't hear them. I only see images: Joan's car, crumpled and mashed, the blue paint chipped. Another car with a bent fender. Police lights round and round and round. I can't see Joan's face. I can't see Ida Red.

"What?" I say. I haven't heard. I know I haven't. I can't see his face through the pictures in my mind.

"She's in the hospital. Let me take you."

Hospital means bed. White sheets. Red blood. Now I see Joan, pale curves. Belly rising from her, the curved dome of skin. Joan's nightmare. Mine too.

———◆◆◆———

"We're very sorry, Mrs..." The doctor looks at his sheet. "Maggie. The damage was extensive. We're doing our best."

There is more he says, but I don't hear. I am looking through the operating window, at the nurses and doctors working there. At the blood on the sheet, spreading across the curve of Joan's belly.

I am looking at the creature in the corner. Its big head, wide mouth. It looks like it's grinning, bloodied lips and chin, tossing something between its teeth. I think it's an apple at first, a tiny red and white thing that crunches and shatters.

It is not an apple.

———◆◆◆———

Joan is not Joan in this hospital room. She is an empty body, an empty belly and limbs and tubes beneath sheets. The beep-beep of her heart and her eyes closed tight.

I sit and I sit and nothing changes. Her breathing doesn't tell me anything, steady as machines. There is nothing to feel as I sit next to her, except her pulse, which never alters. Without her there, saying, "Kiss me," saying "Come to bed," I am afraid to touch her. If she's in there, she's panicking already. I can't make it worse, even though I want to put my hands against her cheek, to touch her now concave belly, to rest my forehead against her neck and weave my fingers into her hair.

When the bearer comes, as I knew it would, it stands in the corner, snorting and snuffling. The sound echoes against the machines.

"No," I say. "No. You had one already. You are full." It chokes me to say this, to have this image of Ida Red in my head while I force the words to come.

The creature shakes its head with a chomp of long teeth. There is something still caught between the bottom canines, a darkening bit of crimson. It takes a step forward, farther into the room, nearing the foot of the bed. I rise and move between it and Joan. I am afraid so hard I can feel it in my hair and in the shake of my knees.

"You can't have her," I say.

It stares at me from across the tiny space. Those black, unseeing eyes. It lifts its head toward the bed, nostrils flaring.

I go down on my knees until I am eye to eye with it. The creature and I stare at each other for a long time. It licks its lips with a dark-red tongue, drags it across those pointed teeth.

Joan's heartbeat beeps through the machine. I think of Ida Red and the way our hands met on Joan's belly, a protective roof over our daughter. I remember the taste of soft chicken and rice on my tongue. I think of her saying, "Don't forget to shower," and the way I never forgot.

Behind me, the sound of the machine slows and slows. Beat. Beat. Beat.

Then nothing.

"No," I whisper. "No."

I know what it needs, what it wants. On my knees, I curve my arms into a circle around my belly, make a soft, dark space in my center.

It comes for me, faster than I could have imagined, and buries its head between my curled arms. It sinks its mouth into what I have offered it, and it bites down.

ONE~WOMAN TOWN

YOU COULD HEAR THE SLINGER COMING FROM miles out, her voice washing 'cross the desert flats like breath whistling across the lip of a bottle. It seeped through the leather and wood of the walls, bending every man's ear in the bar. Some of them started weeping right away. Others paid their tabs fast, pulling their hats down low over their heads as though that would keep their ears safe.

It wasn't just that her song made them sad. It was that they could imagine the beauty of her from the sound of her voice. Terrible beauty always makes men hot and wet and scared. Lust and tears and fear. Combine that with our town's scarcity of women and you've got a dangerous concoction. The men have my boys at their disposal, of course, but we haven't had many real women in Pallaver since the Asuwang, that demon dog, showed up in oh-twenty. The women who didn't get eaten by that black dog hightailed it to safer parts. All except Annie202, who's metal everywhere except her eyeballs and her hair.

Oh, and me, of course. And the only metal I had was a single tin hoop in my left ear and a double-barreled rattlegun behind the bar.

Coming closer, the song turned a loop, rejoined itself on the chorus. Cassidy Jane, one of my boys, came hauling ass down the stairs in his petal-pink dress, his dolled-up eyes so big around they were mostly white. He was the defacto leader of the boys, not because of brawn – skinny little thing with a wasp waist that required me to tie his dresses up with a double ribbon – but because he was never afraid.

"Miss Caroline?" he asked.

"Up," I said. "Warn the others."

He fled back up the stairs, silk train trailing on the wood, jade bracelets jangling on his arm. I hoped they made it through this. Earplugs and roll-ons were the two things I required them to have with them at all times. If they were smart, they were already stuffing their ears. But then again, I hadn't picked my boys for their smarts.

The song grew louder, a woven spellstream that would have beckoned even the best-loved man, would have turned his head right around. Across the bar, Old Man Charlie, whose age is a matter of mystery and pride for him, if for no one else, kept his chin on his cello. He's deaf as a doorpost, but he knows the look on a man's face when trouble's blowing into town.

I gave Charlie a nod, mostly to thank him for staying. Then I took Susan's portrait down from its hanging spot. There weren't a lot of things I cared about saving, but Susan's black-and-white was one of them. I'd only had two years with her before the Asuwang took her – she was its last, a hurried, regrettable mess of a kill – but two years with the right woman can fill a lot of empty heart.

Once I'd gotten Susan safely squared away, wrapped up in a couple of bar towels and tucked under the till, I took Crybaby out of her cradle and settled the gun in the crook of my arm. Cry was mostly for dealing with wandering creepy-crawlies, but she sometimes did double-duty when we had real trouble rolling into town – and this songslinger was sounding more and more like real trouble. There was a lot of power rolled up in those soft-sung notes.

At least the upstairs was quiet, so I knew the boys had done the smart thing – finished up their services, spread around the earplugs, and hunkered beneath the covers with their patrons. We had a lockbox on the stairs between here and there that Annie was wired to set remotely at the first sight or sound of trouble, but I didn't want her to flip the switch until I knew what was what.

The door banged open and the song came in, so thick and woven it was visible in the air, colored with blood. The same color as the slinger's dress, which wrapped around her thick and tight as hair. She was all lily skin, pure alabaster, a color I hadn't seen on a living creature since I'd been a Loyal in Herself's long-ago Court.

The slinger had Annie's head in one hand, holding it by the hair. Wires snapped and crackled at Annie's neck. One of Annie's mismatched human eyes was missing; only the brown one remained. Damn. There went my security system and my only semi-female companion. If I made it out of this alive, I was damn well going to make sure Cry got a chance to rectify that loss.

The slinger came across the floor, more gliding walk than flying. Almost human-like. It's hard for unnatural creatures to manage that. She'd been alive a long time, then. Didn't give a single look to Charlie in the corner. Headed straight for me until she was close enough that I could see her square pupils inside her silver eyes, close enough that I could hear her breath, a half-whistled song through a blade of grass. As she came, she smiled softly, pity and promise, her pointed teeth a hundred rows deep.

Beautiful doesn't begin to say what she was. Neither does deadly. If I didn't have people counting on me, if I hadn't come as far as I had to be who and what I was right now, I would easily have gone on my knees in front of her, begged her to do whatever she wanted to me. And that was without her music bending my will.

Instead I said, "Songslinger." Which is what everyone knows you say to songslingers. They like to be acknowledged. And then you can go on to say the things that really need to be said, which is what I did. "You walk into my bar, singing your tune, carrying my friend's head in your hand, you damn well better be carrying equally big things in your heart."

"That one is not human." The slinger lifted Annie's head, but was looking at me. Slingers never tell the truth nor the lie, just something in between enough to make you feel things you haven't felt in a long long time. Dark things scurrying about, emptying themselves into me and me into them.

I cocked Cry. Gritted my teeth.

"Sister," she said, and she said it in song. "The things we carry, they are too heavy for a hundred hearts."

I never was gladder that Charlie couldn't hear a damn thing. Because as soon as she said that, I knew. I shook my head, like to shake it all away, but still I knew.

Not letting go of Cry with my shooting hand, I poured myself a one-handed shot of distill and then another. I would have offered her one, but slingers don't drink. And on top of that, I hadn't forgiven her for Annie yet. At least she'd had the decency to set Annie's head on one of the stools instead of on the floor. There are monsters and then there are monsters.

I leaned my elbows on the bar top, my throat burning, the crook of Cry resting in my arms like a sleeping babe. A deadly sleeping babe pointed right at the slinger's chest. Wouldn't kill her, a shot like that, but it would be enough to knock the wind out of her. For a voice-bitch, that's a dangerous proposition. Still, she looked at me with those silver eyes and she didn't flinch.

"I'm listening," I said, which is a damn scary thing to say to a slinger, even if you are mostly immune. I was pretty sure I was going to have to kill her, but there was only one way I could do that, and it couldn't happen with Charlie sitting here, watching. Besides, I thought maybe I needed to hear what she was going to say first.

"What would you have this one say?" she asked.

Cry felt perfect in my hands. "How did you find me?"

"Herself has strong-nosed hounds."

"Herself is dead." I wanted another shot of distill, but that was akin to backing down, so I fiddled with Cry's safety latch, the hollow clicks of sound.

"So is that one." Her chin pointed to Annie. I got the message. Resurrected. Or something like it. I might have known. A hundred and eighty years since I'd killed Herself, and she'd been old – but not weak, never weak. Always had a hundred mechanisms in place to prevent failure. Failure, of course, being death. Permanent.

I hadn't noticed it before. The slinger had fooled me with the dress – red was never Herself's color. It was always white and white again. But now that I could see the make, the material, the hundred buttons up both sides, I knew that the dress – and the creature in it – was Herself's.

"And you are here because...?" I clicked Cry's safety off. I thought I knew that answer, at least. But there was a lot that had happened in nearly two centuries. Herself didn't know who I was now. What I was. I wasn't going back, no matter if she came all the way across two worlds to get me.

The slinger took so long to answer I was about to shoot her anyway; the tension and the wait were making my finger shaky on the trigger. She shifted and her crimson dress slid around her like a living thing. A song pulled up and flowed out of her lips, sweet and sorrow. This time, I recognized it for the lullaby that it was and steeled myself against it. But she shook her head, showed the song wasn't for me. So I kept Cry cradled and waited to see what she wanted me to see.

Reaching inside the low V'd neckline of her dress, she pushed the fabric aside to show the alabaster curves of her breasts. It took me a moment to take that in; the only breasts I saw these days were the built ones beneath my boys' dresses and, of course, my own, which I'd had so long I barely noticed.

Along the inner curve of one, no bigger than a grown woman's thumb, latched an alabaster spider. Metallic and jointed. All eight legs sunk into the slinger's skin. It had Herself's head with a hundred white eyes.

I couldn't help myself. I shivered right there, a thing that ran through me from my boots up through the rest of me until it clanked my teeth together hard and made my vision go soft. I'd worn a white widow like that once, when I was Loyal. My every move recorded and relayed, my every word and sigh potential for my own death. Even after I'd torn it from my skin, I'd borne its scars a long, long time.

As the slinger sang, the creature's eyes fell closed, one by one, folding to black. When there was no white left, the slinger covered the creature back up. "The winding web offers a hundred ways to be enthralled," she said.

I looked at her a long time. She looked at me a long time. And we – one who'd once been Loyal by choice and now was something very different and one who was once something free and now was Loyal by bind – we saw each other true.

———◆———

"How much time do we have?" I asked.

The waver in her song gave me all the answer I needed.

I gave up spit-swearing long ago, part of a broken promise that I hadn't been the one to break. But my tongue almost took the world to task with that news.

Instead, I posed the question that had been

haunting me ever since I'd heard that Herself was alive, even since I understood that the slinger had seen through me since the moment she walked in the door. "Does she know about... " A hesitation. "Me?"

A head shake.

"That's some good news, then."

"It is why I came to you," she said, the words looped into her lullaby, keeping the widow at her chest well asleep. But it was only a matter of time before that, too, made Herself suspicious. We were going to have to work fast.

"Keep that bad girl asleep," I said. "And tell me everything you know."

By the time she was done, I had something that looked like a plan. Or the long-lost cousin to a plan. It was risky and stupid and it was all I had.

But I realized something while she'd been talking: I'd done a lot of wrong in my love, both there and here. Maybe especially here. But I loved this town. These men and boys. Annie. Even Old Man Charlie. And I owed them. More than any of them knew. If I could have gotten out fast, saved them from this, I would have. But Herself was a webweaver and she was spinning light across the worlds, aiming for Pallaver.

"Boys!" I yelled. "Come on down!"

'Course they couldn't hear me. I'd forgotten about that. So I fired Cry into the corner. Even Charlie jumped at that. I emptied the rest of the lead out of Cry then, dumping it on the floor. Nothing but trouble if I left her hanging out, still fully loaded.

"Sorry, baby," I told her as I settled her back under the counter. "You're gonna have to sit this one out."

About a second later, my boys were thundering down the stairs, two at a time. You can put them in antique dresses, paint their faces, teach them how to gasp like a girl in the middle of a fuck, but you can't teach them how to run without sounding like a herd of wild horses.

"Aw, Miss Annie," Cassidy Jane said when he saw her head on the chair.

"We'll get her fixed up," I said. "Right now, I need you all to listen to me." I tried to sound more confident that I felt. I wasn't sure how I felt. Herself – the woman who'd forced my love and loyalty and eventually my hand – was alive. Susan and Annie were dead. Or in Annie's case, close enough. A slinger who'd been enthralled by Herself was standing in my bar.

And then there was me.

I laid out the plan, fast. The boys had some experience with this kind of thing – the banshees a few years back, of course, and I'd had their help with the kelpie who'd ridden in on the monsoon one summer – so they listened well and then went off to do what I'd asked. I sent Annie's head off with Carryon Sam with the instructions to find her body and take her over to Albie Jenkins; the farrier would know how to put her back together. I kept Jane back; he and Charlie had a finger language they used and I needed him to pass my request along to the old man when he woke up.

Then I went upstairs to get ready. I asked the slinger to come with me. I told myself it was because I didn't trust her. But of course, that wasn't the truth.

She said nothing, just followed me up, my boots clunking and that dress of hers swishing along the stairs.

Clothes tell your story more than a book or a
song or a gun ever could. The ones I was taking off
told a hundred stories. The man's shirt, buttoned all
but the top one, told the story of how I didn't want to
be seen as a woman in a one-woman town. The metal
loop in my ear said how even at the same time I
couldn't let go of all my woman-self. Pants cleaned a
thousand times of blood and guts and gore and distill
and tears and fucking and horse hide. Boots carrying
the weight of times now and past: shit and dirt and
sand and vomit and more blood and face powder, all
the things we grind under the walks of our lives.

All gone now. The only thing my body still wore
was the circle of leather and charms that wrapped
my hips. Lifebelt. Birth bead to tie it off. A place left
for the death bead. And between it, my whole life told
in knots and weaves. My mother's death. My becoming a novice in Herself's court. When I became true
Loyal. Killing Herself. Escaping. Arriving in
Pallaver. Loving Susan. Being turned. Susan's death.
If I had time, I would have added the slinger. Finding
out Herself was alive. Killing her again. I had a feeling my last bead was coming, and it was not going to
be chosen by me.

I folded all the clothes I'd taken off, laid them
carefully on the bed. Whatever happened, I didn't
want to buried in what I was about to put on.

The slinger, who'd said nothing except her lullaby, let out a quiet gasp when I pulled the dress out of
the trunk and shook it. White-on-white-on-white.
Herself's colors. Only the hem splattered with a red
mist so fine it looked like it belonged there.

It was all wrong. Herself and Her Loyals wearing
red. Me wearing white. Even my bones knew it was

wrong; they ached deep as I pulled the dress up over my hips. I could hear the boys in their rooms around me, getting ready, and I knew I should hurry, but a ritual is a ritual and a ritual is a hard thing to break. My fingers fumbled with the buttons, and the slinger stepped in to help. I tried not to notice my body reacting to her touch. Who could lust in a moment between life and death? But then I always did lust after the ones who had the power to hurt me most.

I did the rest myself. The woven leggings, still mostly intact. The boots that slid up over my knees. The silver bracelets with the blades hidden in their curves. When I lifted the tearpearl choker from its case, the slinger came forward and took it from my hands.

"That one will bend," she said, and I thought again how telling the truth at slant sometimes told it truer than seemed possible.

I lowered my head, let her wrap my throat in dried tears. She said nothing about the long scars at the back of my neck, across my shoulders, but I knew she knew them. And when I thought I was strong enough to step forward and not fall, I started the trek back down the stairs, the slinger singing at my heels.

———◆◆◆———

The boys outdid themselves. Not just in dresses. They'd dug up enough powder to turn every bit of their skin lily-white, done their lips in rose-petal red. If you didn't look too close, they could have been Loyals. Or Loyals as they'd been once, before Herself had pulled from the grave and turned her color into blood. Well, if she wanted to take red, then I would take white. And I would own it, deserved or not.

The boys had brought the men back too. Men who were looking mighty nervous about being in the same room with a slinger, but who were here nonetheless. They thought they owed me something, that was all. Which made me ache a little. But if I could get them out of this alive, then I would.

I caught a few sideways glances at me, too. It wasn't just the dress – none but one of them had ever seen me in a dress and that had been the day I'd ridden into town. A couple, you could tell, were thinking things they'd not thought about me before.

Charlie and Jane had communicated clearly – Charlie was rosining up his bow good and thick. And the best part was Annie sitting up at the bar, having a shot of something that Albie had mixed up for her. She had one pig's eye and one human's, but she gave a mechanical grin and a thumbs-up when she saw me. Our security system was a go.

I brought out the tiny bottle of perfume I'd saved all those years, gave each of the boys and the men a single drop under their noses.

"She's going to come quick," I said, when they were all sniffing themselves, something that would have been laughable in any other place and time. "Don't let her surprise you."

I gestured to all of them to put their earplugs in and when they had, I reached forward and took the slinger's hand. I didn't mean to do that last bit, and in a hundred years and in a hundred stories I couldn't tell you what made me do it. But I took her hand in front of all those people that I cared for and I said, "Now."

The slinger cut the lullaby she'd been singing, let

it flow away for half a beat. And then she picked up some new tune, something wild and dangerous. Even I felt it call to me. No one could miss it. Not the men with their pins in, not Annie with her non-human ears, not the widow at the slinger's chest. Not Herself, the White Widow of death who waited on the far side of the sound.

While the slinger sang, we waited. They don't talk about that in the stories they tell – and someone, somewhere was going to be telling this story, although they wouldn't tell it true. The fighting, the shooting, the magic-slinging – those are the easy parts. It's the waiting that kills a man. Or a woman. Especially waiting when you could hear nothing but the heart-whipping beat of the slinger's song, underwritten by Charlie's weeping cello. Men's eyes white all around. Their tense stillness broken only by their shifting. The boys had it a little easier, half-hidden by powder and fabric and glamour.

We wouldn't hear Herself come. Wouldn't see her either, until she wanted us to. But if Herself had one flaw, it was pride. Ego. She would show herself out of vanity before she would try to sink her teeth in me. At least, I hoped she would. I was counting on that.

And show she did. Just when my eyes had gotten shifty and heavy from staring at one spot after another, I felt her hot fanged breath coming down on from above. The smell of soft living things falling to rot. Up on the ceiling she hung by eight crimson furred legs, her wide back bearing its black blade mark. Her invisible web only visible because it was strung with perfect droplets of blood. Uncountable in their numbers.

Her face craned to look down at me, a thousand garnet eyes. My knees wanted nothing more than to fall, to bring me down to where I belonged under that gaze. To bow my head and offer the back of my neck. The slinger sang louder, tightened her hand in mine, and I stayed standing.

From the ceiling, Herself came. And as she came, she changed. Lengthened. Two of her legs becoming something to stand upon, two becoming something akin to hands, sprouting three long, blackened fingers on each. The rest slipped into the depths of her fur that became a dress, soaked three times in blood. Her bracken face elongated into something that resembled humanity no more than Annie's pig-eyed face did. Humanity stopped at her eyes, segmented, off-white as webbing, threaded with strands of dead-tone gray. Nothing flickered there. Nothing ever had, except once the reflection of my love for her. I'd mistaken it for something living.

Herself opened the thing that had become her mouth, rows of rusted copper points splaying mismatched inside her boned lips. She swallowed, adjusted, remade her mouth into lush red – lips and tongue and teeth rouged crimson.

"You think to beat me with my own songstress and this player of wood?" Herself's words hung in the air, stretched out long and low. If the slinger's voice was lips and wings on the wind, Herself's was a beaded string that tightened and pulled. I felt it in the constriction of my own response, the half-swallowed sound of no words.

I drink down the last shot of distill I'd poured earlier. The burn opened my throat enough to get the words out.

"Let's you and me make a deal," I said.

Herself's laugh sounded the way her breath

smelled. Dead that believes it's still alive. Putrid and maggot-ridden and buried and dug up again. Even with the perfume, I could hear a few of the men gagging, swallowing it back. And yet they couldn't take their eyes from her, couldn't help themselves moving closer to her black beauty. Herself would talk them into their own deaths if I let her.

She laughed again, thick and violent, and the movement whispered along her web. The droplets of blood stirred, stretched. No, not droplets. Not blood. Herself's creatures. They needed only seconds to waken fully. Soon they would rouse themselves to become an army of Loyals, dressed in red, fanged and knived. Innumerable daughters, born for nothing more than the protection of their ruler.

"No," she said. Simple as that. Just as I had told them she would.

All around me, I heard the lockboxes go click. Annie, doing the work of a thousand for me, and I had to smile a little. Whoever died in here or lived, those boxes would keep all otherworld creatures here, trapped. At least long enough for word to get out and people to prepare.

Charlie's cello began to dance, the slinger weaving her song into it. The tune was fast and hard, enough to shake the web, shake the thousand red drops from their high safety. My boys were quick. They bent in their dresses and went at the Loyals with their knives, stabbing them even as they fell. I felt a quick pang of pride at seeing the boys, my boys, on their knees, spattering their dresses with blood.

Herself watched them for a second, half-turning so that I could see her profile, the shifting space of skin and fur, the poisonous mouth that refused to hide its weapons. She could take out my boys with little more than a meatstink word. They were just here for diversion. I was using them yet again, and they thought it was all for them.

"Listen," I said to her over the music. "I am yours. If you leave the town be."

It is not only slingers who can slant the truth.

Herself turned. She came to me. Of course she did. Who can resist their lusts, their love? She slipped across the floor, bringing her stench with her, the power of her deaths rolling off her in a red wash.

"My Once Loyal," she said. "My Once Love."

I lowered my eyes, let her think it was deference. Who knows what she might have seen of herself in my reflection. Her hand reached up to touch my cheek, and I swallowed back the bile that rose, hot and choking.

"Kiritsanu."

From her mouth, the name that had once been mine still bore power over me, somehow. I had not expected that. A room full of Loyals, full of boys and men and song and love, closed in just her and me and that name I'd once worn, once promised to be Loyal to.

I am Miss Caroline, I tried to whisper, but that name was so young, it had so little power. I tasted the hot bile of her breath and it sang sweet on my tongue.

The slinger's hand slipped away from mine, and I let it. Somewhere far off, I heard a song, a call to wake and be woken. I couldn't listen. I belonged to Herself. I was Loyal. I was...

"Miss Caroline," I heard Jane say. Real or imagined, I didn't know. But it was enough for me to find a small thread of real, to hold onto it tight. I stayed still. I needed Herself close, closer. The boys took up the name, bless them, repeated it over and over. My own Loyals, doing their best to save me.

"My true," she said. "Be true again." This first a whisper.

"Despite your little plan, I will kill them all." This second a promise.

There was no way she would spare them. Not whether I lived or died.

Against all my wishes, against all my fears, I bowed my head fully, let her see the back of my neck, exposed except for the single strand of tears that covered it. The scars of her fangs, criss-crossed, unhealed. She hissed, a sound of desire and greed.

No matter what else she was, she was female, woman. I could smell it in her blood and breath and skin, the lust that preceded everything she'd been and would become.

I was Miss Caroline. But I was something else, something more recent. I closed my eyes and called to the creature in myself, the one I'd buried so long ago. I'd had no control back then, no power over the thing that had come to me in the night. But then I had taken the woman that I'd loved. And I'd fought the creature inside me for a hundred days until I'd captured hold of it and caged it forever in the empty ribcage of my chest.

Now, I hoped I could do the one thing I'd promised never to do – bring it back.

Gripping the front of my neck with her too-hot hand, Herself bent over me, beginning to whisper the words that would seal us again, skin to blood.

"Close your eyes," I said. Not to Her. To the ones

I loved. I wanted to spare them, I always did, but it was too late. Too late. Always my curse. They couldn't hear me over the music, over the sound of knives against leatherwood, but they would see it all.

Herself's fangs broke my skin and I broke with it. It was so easy, too easy, and it scared me for half a beat before it took me over completely.

Where there once was a woman in white grew a monster too long caged. Hungry for flesh and blood. A creature of shadow and blood and lust. Black-as-night dog with crimsoned wings. I knew my own eyes, their red-rimmed madness. Knew the stink of my own silvered fangs.

"I knew," Herself said. Her laughter the stench of death come home to roost.

Too late for me to turn away. Too late for me to save them. Or me. Growling, I sank my fangs into the edge of her throat, my claws tearing roughshod across her bowed abdomen. She was cold where she should have been hot, crumbled to dust where she should have been meat. And still I tore, wild, starving.

Herself screamed once, wild and true, and then she said no more.

Herself had known. All this time, all this way, she'd known. Of course she had. Each of us, in the end, craves the thing we promise we do not want.

Silence beat back the sound of breath, the sound of gasp, even the sound of song.

After a long time, someone – it might have been Jane – whispered my true name.

Asuwang.

I looked up, and saw myself reflected in their open-eyed gazes.

Everywhere there was crimson and silence. The boys had their knives, Charlie and the slinger had their songs, Annie had locked the exits against me. Cry was empty behind the bar, far out of my reach. Upstairs, my clothes folded, my death bead on the top. I'd armed the ones I loved with everything they needed.

Now there was nothing to do but wait.

FORCED EXPIRATION

HIS WIFE HAS BEEN HERE FOR FORTY DAYS. The machines make her heart beat and her lungs whoosh, a steady metronome of blood and air. You could try to count the future out, minutes on the rise of her chest, hours on the fall of it.

I know that's what he's doing, the way he keeps the flat of his palm on the flat of her chest, somewhere between lung and heart. The way his gray sky eyes watch the back of his hand rise and fall, rise and fall. Counting.

He is here every morning. Evenings too. Sitting in that plastic hospital chair in the same pair of jeans, that same gray cable-knit sweater that matches his eyes. His wife, with her dark hair tucked behind her ears and flat brown eyes staring upward, almost looks more alive than he does. Even the long-dead flowers behind him, their golden petals dark and stained, still reach skyward.

I've asked the regular nurses if he goes home at night, and although they would like to pretend I am not here, would like to rip my white scrubs right off and press them to black beneath their nurse's shoes, they answer me, as they must. Yes, he goes somewhere.

I don't believe it. They tell me lies sometimes, in the hope that I will not be needed. That I will go away.

If someone is taking him at night – sister, buddy, son – then they need to start feeding him; his cheekbones, the point of his chin, show sharp through his brown stubble, and the dirty sweater slides off his thinning shoulders.

When I step into the room with him, I do it with strong shoes against squeaky floors, loud enough so he can hear me coming, quiet enough that I don't mess up his count. He almost looks at me as I near the bed, but really he just raises his chin. What's left of thirty years of good manners in a time like this.

I slide my stethoscope off my neck, press the metal diaphragm to warm against my palm.

"I'm just going to check her vitals," I say. Really, I don't need to. This many machines in a person and you can read their whole life story in the blips: BP 80 over nothing, pulse thready, even with the machine, future flat.

But I will check anyway. I am supposed to keep my hands on my patients. That's my job. Well, that's my pseudo-job. That's what the hospital administrators will tell you if you ask them. The other nurses too, although if you caught them three martinis down and offered anonymity, then who knows?

Most of the time, the hospitals wish I didn't exist. The nurses too – I know they think it's blasphemous that I wear white scrubs, like a pregnant woman going down the aisle all in white. But when things start to fall apart, I'm the one they call.

Yes, I am a nurse, and, I believe, a good one. But not to this woman. My patients are the people sitting in these plastic chairs counting heartbeats and breaths. My patients are the Loved Ones. The Lo's.

My job is to keep the Lo's sane, to keep them alive however I can while they're sitting here, counting on dying. One of the ways I do this is by letting them see my hands taking care. I make the motions of checking his wife's BP, roll her eyelids up and shine my light on her dark brown centers. Pupils, dilated, non-responsive. I put two fingers against her pulse, wrap my hands around her wrist. But I don't count. There is nothing here worth counting on.

While I take care with my hands, I take stock of my real patient, with my eyes. His vitals are: Sweater gray, energy gray, eyes gray. The hand just above his wife's feeding tube, gray. More gray than his wife's skin. More gray than the hospital sheets before they are bleached back to nearly white.

He moves his eyes to my hands when I peel back the tape inside his wife's elbow, check the skin where the silver IV needle sits. Her flesh is cool and slightly purple beneath my fingers. Already her skin is falling down into itself, plummy and cell-less.

Sometimes, I can turn a light on in a Lo's eyes or have them lean forward to ask a question, if I'm rough enough. But not this one. His eyes are clouds torn by wind. Lighting might kill him. I stroke the inside of her elbow and watch for a reaction. But his hand stays on her chest, trapped between white sheet and air, counting the rise, the fall.

Unlike the other nurses, I don't ask Lo's how

they are doing or how they feel. They'll say, "fine" or "okay" if they say anything at all. To say or think otherwise would admit defeat. Instead, I ask something calculable, something with numbers and a rhythm. What's your home phone number? What is your insurance company? How old is she? On what date did you first notice the symptoms?

For him, I will ask, "How many?" But not yet, not until I'm sure he doesn't know.

———◆◆◆———

When I come back the next morning, I am sure. He has both hands on her chest and doesn't lift his chin when I stand next to the bed. Where his thin arms poke from the sweater sleeves, his skin is rippled with goose bumps. He is doubling up his count, sure that soon she is going to recover or she is going to die. He is preparing himself for these possibilities. Rise or fall.

He does not yet understand that there is a third option, the one her body has chosen, the one that is so long he will never be able to count on it. He is the only one who doesn't understand that she is not, never, coming out of it.

This is what patients in vegetative states do. Like mermaids with land legs, they convince their loved ones that they're not drowning, no, they're swimming up and up. Just hang on to them, just hold their hands and follow their breathing – they will take you to the surface. The truth is they're just floating half-way between bottom and surface, holding their loved ones down with them for as long as possible. It's not the patients' fault; they don't know they're doing it. Like the mermaids, their beauty captures the Lo's, holds them captive. It is my job to break them free.

I put my hand next to his on the sheet without touching him. I've heard photographers say that when they're setting up for a shoot, they exhale and click the photo right at the moment their lungs are empty. It makes their shots steadier.

For Lo's who are counting, I wait until the patient inhales, because the inhale takes longer, because it doesn't mess up their count.

Her breath, the mechanical suck of it, in and in.

"How many?" I ask.

He doesn't lift his gray eyes. Below our hands, the body of his wife exhales. Inhales.

He runs the dry tip of his tongue across the skin of his top lip. It makes the sound of a dead leaf on the sidewalk. Hiss. Suck.

"Today," he says. Whoever's taking him home at night isn't making him talk. His voice scrapes out, rusty. He doesn't clear his throat. Another inhale. "Three hundred and sixty-two."

I slide my hand across the sheet, across the waves that are the ribs of his wife, until my pinky finger touches the side of his. His knuckle is split open down the side, a recent wound not cared for, the edges of it sharp against my skin.

Matching his wife, I take my own inhale. The air is heavy with discarded pieces of body and breath.

"How many more?" I ask.

He doesn't know. He thinks the number is still calculable, that there is an equation in his head that he must figure out.

His pinky twitches against mine, a dry twig. I

know he would pull his hands back if he could, but he can't. He cannot miss a breath, a count. He thinks he is almost to the end.

I press my pinky tighter to his skin, to that wound.

"How many?"

This time, his finger stays steady against mine. His eyes are back on his hands, gray on gray on white. He is counting inside his mouth, 364, 365... I have lost him.

How many more? If I could answer for him, I would. I would say *pi more*. I would say *irrational number more*. I would say *forever more*.

Instead, I take my hand away and unwrap my stethoscope from its home around my neck. For now, all I can do is let him see me taking care.

———◆———

The next morning, I tell the day nurse in charge that we need to schedule surgery for his wife. Coming from me, she knows what this means. Transport the patient somewhere else for a few hours so I can work. It doesn't mean she likes it. She pulls a pencil from her gray and black ponytail, looks at me hard for a few seconds, her blue eyes like steel.

"When?" she says.

I run my fingers over the tools in my pocket – circle and square. "Now."

She cradles the black handset between her cheek and shoulder. "Now?"

I know it's asking a lot. I also know she'll do it.

"Thanks," I say. Even though I don't have to. Even though she says nothing back.

He is the same. Thinner maybe. Grayer inside his sweater if that's possible.

"Daniel," I plucked his name from his chart on the way in. I don't usually do that, get involved in a name kind of way. It's like kissing on the lips. But sometimes you have to breathe for them.

I walk around to his side of the bed. Stand beside him without touching him. I explain to him what's going to happen.

His eyes, dead on his hands. His wife, dead, not-dead through machines. He doesn't hear a word. He counts. But I have to say it – hospital regulations. The hospital could get sued for the work I do here; although if it came to that, they'd feed me to the dogs, say they didn't know the type of work I did. It doesn't matter. No one ever sues.

I slide the small needle out of my scrub pocket and pull off the protective cap. When the silver enters the vein in his neck, his skin makes a small pop. He doesn't flinch, not even when the sedative goes in, though I know this one stings through the veins like jellyfish. Still, nothing. I raise my fingers to the crew outside the door, telling them to wait. One breath, two.

Like Ritalin on hyperactive children, the sedative will do the opposite in a few minutes. But right now, he is all rag doll, limp as those big cats they capture on TV. I wait until his hands begin their inevitable slide down the ribcage of his wife's body before I signal the crew in to take away his wife.

His eyes are closed. I have less than five minutes to get him where I need him. I lean down and put his arm around my shoulder. I know enough not to inhale, but still I get his sour milk scent on my tongue.

"Up we go," I say.

I am strong – I have to be – and he is nothing but bones and breath. I almost overshoot and send us both toppling. But I right myself and navigate us through the door and down the hall to the cleaning room. All the way, patients look at us funny – Daniel's left arm sticks straight out, his hand flat like it's been for months. It makes him look as though he's trying to swim through air.

I get Daniel inside the cleaning room, slide him into the chair in front of the large three-headed shower. The sed kicks in just as I slide the deadbolt into the lock. For the first time, his eyes actually see me, see the space around him. Now his eyes are blue, not gray.

"Where..." Again the throat that doesn't work. I turn on one of the showerheads. "Where am I?"

When all three showerheads are spraying behind him, I kneel in front of his chair. The scent of dirt and urine is everywhere in his jeans.

"You're in the hospital. Your wife – "

When I say wife, his eyes go wide and deeper blue. His hands fumble to raise himself.

"Where is she?"

I put one hand on his jeaned knee, try to hold him in the chair with what I can tell him.

"In a procedure." I don't say surgery. Surgery gives them hope, one way or the other. "You couldn't be with her."

Something lets go inside his eyes, blue sky to gray. He lets his head fall to his chest. His hands go flat on his knees. Inside his mouth, he is counting her breaths, letting his own chest rise and fall at the speed he remembers them. He is nearly exact in his timing.

I wait for his inhale.

"You need to start thinking of yourself now," I say. "Get undressed, take a shower."

Exhale, inhale. I need to break him of the habit, but I need to get him into the shower more.

He doesn't want any part of this. He will sit in the chair and count until someone brings him back to his wife, and then he will sit in another chair and count until one of them dies.

I slip a pair of rubber gloves from my scrubs pocket and slide them over my fingers. Then I bend down further and untie his sneakers. The smell of his socks as I pull them off makes me gag and I rise too quickly, feeling my head spin.

"Stand up." I pick him up a second time. He doesn't fight me – he is keeping time. Counting breaths is all that matters. He is showing his wife how much he loves her by keeping the beat of her breath inside his mouth.

My trauma shears slice through the bulky front of the sweater and the dirty t-shirt inside it. His chest is sunk to hollow, his bones everywhere inside his skin.

I put one hand on the button of his jeans.

"Don't make me cut you out of your pants too," I say. He does not hear. Goose bumps break out on his thighs when I pull his dirty jeans down to his feet. His boxers come down easily, too loose now for his waist.

Still in my scrubs, I take his hand and lead him into the showers. When I soap him down, he becomes less gray, takes on the appearance of near human again. My scrubs stick wet to me, turning gray from the dirt and water. Even my gloves are turning a yellow gray, like the sky before a thunderstorm.

I turn him around. Both of his hands are over his heart. I run the bar of soap down his chest, feel his breath in and out. His beat is off now, a little slower than the rhythm the ventilator gives his wife. Still he counts behind the fence of his teeth.

When I reach his belly button, I squat down and start at his feet, work up to his knees. While I take care with my hands, I take stock of my patient with my eyes. Beneath the spray of the hot water, the skin of his shoulders and chest has turned an angry red. It is a good red. An alive red.

I rub the soap over his hips. His penis is still flaccid and tiny. Still gray. Gray penis, gray eyes, gray matter – the last three parts of him to come back to life. The water is in my shoes; they push out gray suds with every step.

I soap up my gloved hand and run it along the inside of his thighs, cup it against the underside of his balls. He makes a sound somewhere in his throat, somewhere in his chest. My soapy fingers reach the base of his penis, circle it, draw long and slow down its soft sides.

This is where it gets tricky. Guilt, fear; there are many reasons a Lo freaks out at this point. I have to move slowly enough that he isn't fully aware of what I'm asking of him, quickly enough that by the time he's aware, it's too late. And I can't speak. To exhale breath with sound would remind him that I am not his wife doing these things, that I am not supposed to be here.

I let his penis fall back against his thigh. It's still gray, but there is some firmness to it now. Then I re-soap my hands and slide the bar into the red Sharps container on the wall. I wrap one gloved hand around the base of his penis, and pull in soft, short tugs with the other. Beneath my hands, everything lengthens and hardens. Everything begins to turn pink.

He doesn't want this. His body, awake and asking for something, anything to stay alive, is betraying him.

"No," he says. "No, no, no..." but it is more moan than words. The sound of someone who has already fallen.

I watch the rhythm of his chest, the numbers that are almost visible behind the gate of his teeth, and go opposite. Short then long. Stroke, stroke, stop. Anything to get him off the rhythm of his wife's chest. Anything to make him stop counting. Anything to break the hold of the infinite numbers and keep him alive.

I keep my fist moving, back and forth in a rhythm with no pattern, something so humanly erred that no machine could follow. Something that is impossible to count. He still tries, though. I can see it in his teeth, gnashed together to keep everything inside. I stop stroking, cup my hand again beneath his balls. I wait, one beat, two, two and a half. And then I pick up the rhythm again, fast fast against his reddening skin. So fast he could not count it if he tried.

He leans back against the wall of the shower. His palms are flat against the tile, his eyes closed. He pumps his hips forward and back, forward and back. It is a rhythm, but it is not the rhythm of his wife's breath. It is his own rhythm. It is the beat of his own life, returning. He has let go of the mermaid's hand and begun to kick toward surface.

When he comes in my hands, he is crying. I strip off my gloves with their palms full of gray fluid and drop them into the Sharps container. Then I lean in and put my arms around him. The water washes over us in its fierce rhythm, rinsing him clean, driving the gray further into the fabric of my scrubs.

Right now, he lets me hold him because he lost the only thing he had to hold on to and I seem something like the surface. In a few hours, when he sees his wife again and he tries to put his clean hands on her chest, he will remember it was me who took her away. And years from now, when his wife has been here for so long that her breaths are more numerous than the stars, and he has gone on with his life, he might try to find me. He might try to thank me. But I'll be long gone, on to other places where they count on me to take care.

THE LURE OF
DANGEROUS WOMEN

WE HAD TO MOVE INLAND AFTER THE INCIDENT. That's how we call it. "The incident." A euphemism of denial. The worst kind of lie.

In New Orleans, there was too much water, too many wet and unfettered places. Too much of the dark stink carried in the fall of the rains, the dank wood at the back of bars. Sometimes, when the rivers rose and the bayou broke against the dams, I dreamed of skin beneath my hands, shimmering, shimmering, singing almost, as the curves strained and fell against the touch of my fingers. If I could close my eyes and hear the growled break of her voice washing over my skin, along the curves of my chest and hips, rivering though the empty space between my thighs.

Michelle dreamed of other things, I knew, from the way her voice caught in her throat in sleep, spilled forth between clenched teeth, nonsense words in a shored-up, lyrical language. Nonsense words, but anyone could hear the stutter, the bone-deep pain in their sharp sounds.

How much blame do I take? I'm never sure. After all, I was the one who found her – if you believed 'her' was the right term, which some days I did, but mostly I didn't. I'd came upon her in a New Orleans dive, as easy as if she had picked me out of the crowd and was beckoning, was singing, just for me. As if it was predestined. Maybe it was. Or maybe I tell myself that so I won't feel so bad, so my heart won't dry up and crack open under the weight of blame.

Michelle and I had moved to NOLA, a temporary stay, right after the big flood, so Michelle could work – she was on the film crew for a documentary series. She spent her days documenting the destruction – land, lives, legacies, while I spent my waking hours shiftless and jobless. I taught painting classes back home, but I'd decided to take a break, come with her. I thought maybe a new place would get me painting again. So far, it hadn't happened.

"It's fine," she said more than once about my lack of job, kissing my forehead, the side of my mouth, her breath smelling of coffee and,– dangerously for me – of prawns. "We don't need the money."

But I needed something to keep me afloat. Or, perhaps, to keep me from floating off. From losing myself in the unanchored drift of New Orleans life. I couldn't partake in the local seafood – a near-death-like allergic reaction to shrimp when I was twenty had made me cautious about anything that lived in water, despite how much I missed the flavor of clams and oysters, how much I ached to have the butter-meat of scallops and lobster between my teeth. I wasn't much of a drinker, either. Not a gambler or a girl-whore – Michelle and I had been seriously monogamous from the start, a situation that seemed to be working, despite the fact that it was new for both of us.

So what was there to do but prowl the streets, listening to the musicians, finding places to introduce Michelle to once the sun settled down in its watery bed? She loved music. I loved music too, but in a visceral, pulse-speeding way that I couldn't have explained if I'd tried. Michelle loved music in a way that was knowledgeable and clinical, from how the bones in our ears heard sound to the reason New Age music appealed (something about a heartbeat-like rhythm). She'd once done a documentary on great classical players, and she'd tried to explain to me what made one good and another bad, but I could only say, "I like that one." Or, "That one makes my head feel all jangly." It became my daily goal to find a place or a band or a single, hidden gem of a musician that would make her sink into her seat, dark hair curling up against her face in the heat, giving me that small half-smile of hers across the dark bar, mouthing, "Good find" to me beneath the pulse of the music. And then later, our desire heightened by the music, she'd pull me back to our extended-stay hotel, laughing and swinging her hips, pushing me down onto the bed, tongue dragging along my mouth like a cat, like I was irresistible – cream.

——◆◆◆——

Despite the aimlessness of my day-to-day life there, I liked New Orleans. Liked the dirt of it, the cheesiness of it. The tourist bars, the two-for-one, the girls in their beads – all these were the first things to come back, as though flashing a magic-markered beer sign and a bit of boob were all it retook to build a city. Even the voodoo was cheesy. All those shrunken heads wearing Mardi Gras crowns, as though they were giving you a nudge-nudge and a wink-wink.

The scent in those weeks following the flood could be massive when the wind turned. Things brought from the depths of lakes and ponds, hundred- and thousand-year old entities that had never seen the light of day. The air smelled of algae and the dirty maws of creatures and of long-rotting bodies dumped in the dark of night. And even that didn't turn me away from the city I was coming to love. Something about it seemed right, natural. It meshed with the false fullness in everyone's cheeks, the frenzy in their eyes, as though they were trying to bring themselves, and the city, back to life just by their very willpower.

I liked that sometimes Michelle worked late into the evening, filming in the dark, and I could walk the streets and alleyways alone, savoring the way they took on a whole new feel, a pulsing heartbeat of tourists and music and sex. The girls didn't turn my head, but then I never felt they were there for me, always eyeing the guys, casting their lures to drag them in. Quiet, easy catches: college fratters and unhappily married old men seemed to be their easiest prey.

We'd been there nearly two weeks when Michelle came back late to the hotel, wrecked and weeping.

She was not much of a weeper, truly. At least not for herself. But the white around her big dark eyes was threaded with red, and I knew she'd been at it a while. It happens with her, around the half-way point of any tough documentary, and I'd been expecting it, to be honest. It's when they start editing. Michelle could watch anything through a lens and barely blink – it's why she's so good at what she does – but after, when she had to re-see it, I know it tears at her.

I waited while she stripped off her jeans and boots – muddied and caked with who knew what – and let her shower away as much of the day as she could. I stood on the hotel balcony while she dressed; when you're a couple living in a hotel room, even a nice hotel room paid for by the company, there's never enough privacy. I didn't want to go too far, in case she needed to talk, but I didn't want to be in her face either.

"Beth?" I turned toward where she was leaning against the doorway. Long dark hair damp and curling up around her shoulders, her shoulders still wet from the shower. She was wrapped in my bathrobe, the mint green of the silk all wrong for her olive skin, but it didn't matter. I wanted her with the urgency of surfacing, of needing to breathe after having been under too long.

"Come to bed with me?" she asked. And I felt a breeze of relief. It wasn't one of the really bad ones, then. I nodded, and took her hand and pulled her back into the room, toward the ridiculously oversized king size bed that I'd begun to think of as 'ours.'

Michelle's a sweet lover. All tongue, no teeth, is how I used to describe it to friends, teasing her. But it was good that way; her hard body in contrast to her soft touch always got me off, always left me arching into her for more.

But this time, she barely let me get on the bed before she was digging her fingers into me, hard. Her skin felt too dry beneath my fingers, too broken up, as though it would crumble and slip away if I held on too hard. Her aggressiveness was unusual, but I was so swept under by the sudden clench of her fingers, by the beating of her thumb against me, that I couldn't think. Couldn't do anything but call her name into the air, *Chelle* and *Chelle* and *Chelle*, so that it was crashing through me, as caressing and killing as the sea.

———◆◆◆———

"Beth..." she said, after. Her cheek rested to the curves of my chest. Her drying hair curled around the play of my fingers.

"Mhn?" I thought that maybe when this was over we'd take a vacation, somewhere warm and sandy. She could take a break between movies – she always was working too hard – and maybe I'd paint again. Find something in the beaches that moved my hands into action.

"Let's do a baby. I can try this time."

I itched suddenly for a cigarette, and I had to close my eyes to keep from seeing her face, the broken blood vessels that lined her eyes from crying. "Fuck, Michelle."

Every couple has its points of contention, I know. Some worse than others. We had this. Most of the time we put it away, buried beneath sand and rock, where it sat, quiet and easily ignored. And then something – waves, dog, creature – would dig it up and we'd find ourselves looking at it. Dirty, decayed thing. A thing we'd been over again and again.

I moved away from her as much as I could without actually moving away. She pushed her head forward, resting it on my stomach, her fingers reaching to play in the short curls between my legs. "Baby, it won't be like the last times. I know it won't. Maybe we should try me this time."

I had a sudden urge to slap her hand away, and I gritted my teeth, saying nothing, a sharp pain pushing up through my stomach in memory.

She saw something in my flinch. "It wasn't your fault," she said. "It wasn't your fault."

And she sounded so much like an after-school special, like a badly cast school therapist patting the heroin-strung teen on the head, that I did something I've never done before. I lifted myself from the bed and got dressed and I left her, curled there, naked and open-mouthed. The best I could do was growl out a "I'm going for a walk" before I shut the door.

———————

That was the night I found her. I wanted cigarettes, wanted them bad. I'd quit at Michelle's urging back before we tried to get pregnant, but now that was all over; my body having rejected the thing I'd wanted and wanted, I'd taken to sometimes having a smoke in the evenings. A single, slow-puffed reminder of something I'd loved once that was no longer good for me. Now, I wanted a pack. To be able to inhale the mingled smoke and air at my leisure. To say, if only temporarily, "Fuck it."

I stepped out onto Marion Street with my cigarettes, packing them against my palm – a motion that never goes away, I don't think, no matter how long it's been since you've done it. The wind turned, bringing with it the funk of the water and bodies and that strangely sour-and-sweet scent of the bayou. And it brought the sound of her voice too. Ragged, broken, like she'd been smoking a few too many cigarettes herself, but wild and feral, a growl of the blues that sank through my ears down into the space between my thighs, still aching and wet from Michelle's fingers.

Stopping still, I flicked my lighter against the paper end of a cigarette, cocking my head toward the music. I had one of those sudden glimpses of how I looked from the outside – hair sex-tousled and in need of a cut, dressed in jeans and a men's t-shirt, scowling, inhaling desperately from a cigarette while I listened, entranced, to just another washed-up singer cranking the blues down the street. It was the first time I'd wanted to paint anything since I'd gotten here, and what I wanted to paint was me. Me in the act of listening to her.

Then the moment passed and I was just me, inside myself. Lifting my head, I realized I was at the intersection of the hotel and the bar, and I could take a right, turn back to Michelle. Throw away the pack of smokes on the way. Make nice.

But I knew I didn't want to. I wanted to find the voice, to sit in a dark and smoky room, filling an ashtray with butts, losing myself in the rugged purr of her.

She wasn't hard to find – her voice carried

through the streets and caressed me, guided me like a native to her place. I slipped in and took a seat in the back. The bar, like so many in New Orleans, was just right for hiding in. Poorly lit, half-full of men who'd had enough drinks that they'd forgotten they didn't know how to dance, girls in next-to-nothing, offering sugary shots from test tubes tucked in their chests.

But it was the stage that captured me. No, not the stage. Her, on it. Dressed in flowing green pants that curved around her hips, flowed around her legs as she moved in time to the band. A tight, shimmery shirt – black or grey – that showed off a strip of smooth belly beneath the hem and cap sleeves that did nothing to hide her arms. Strong, lean. Swimmer's arms that held the mic while she swayed, lush as seaweed, rocking in tune to the music of the seas.

And her voice, ah, god, her voice. Didn't matter what she sang – oldies, blues, a pop request from the drunken guy trying to stand at her feet – she crooned and cranked, a sound that I could feel not just in the hammer and anvil and stirrup of my ears, but in every bone in my body. My femur and radius, my clavicle and pelvis. I don't know how long I sat. An older man who was trying to kiss the singer's feet was rewarded with a choke-hold from one of the bouncers and was led out the door. The couple off to the right of me started making out; she was nearly under the table with her head in his lap. But none of this really held my attention. I watched her move through the gray screen of my cigarette smoke and I listened and listened.

At some point, she let the band take over – the guitarist sang and she slipped off the stage with a bucket for tips. The guitarist had a good voice, but the energy changed. People turned away from the stage, ordered drinks, slipped outside to find another bar. It seemed I wasn't the only one enraptured by her.

She carried her tip bucket around the room, touching people on the arm, leaning in, talking, laughing. I watched, smoking, hoping she'd come to me, hoping she wouldn't. I was suddenly nervous, and fumbled in my pocket for cash to put in her bucket.

When she reached me, she leaned in, whispering, but I couldn't hear above the guitarist's yell. Tucking a finger into my ear, she pressed at the front of it, which somehow shut out all the music without shutting out her voice. Her fingertip was cool despite the heat. There was something so sensual in that touch that I nearly had to close my eyes. It felt wrong to be touched by her, too much, as though she wasn't supposed to be this close to humanity, surrounded by the stink and filth.

"Anything special you want, love?" she asked, that hoarse and perfectly ruined voice, her lips moving against my ear.

And God help me, I couldn't answer. I couldn't give her one single thing. I could only shake my head, blushing like a schoolgirl. Mute.

She laughed as though she'd seen it before. "Don't worry, baby," she said. Her fingertip slid down my neck, following the river of my throbbing pulse. "I know what you want to hear."

———◆———

Michelle was asleep when I got home, sprawled on top of the covers, the ceiling fan buzzing overhead like a swarm of flies. The light was nearly up by then, a hazy gray batten of clouds flowing like dirty water across the sky. I don't remember getting home so much. I knew I stank of whiskey and cigarettes, of muck water and fetid, damp air. In the odd light, my skin wore a green-gray hue of the undernourished and over-alcoholed.

I slid in beside Michelle and despite my throbbing head, I could see her again for all that she was. My Chelle, my music-lusting, film-maker, big-hearted lover. I put my arm over her and she wiggled closer without waking. But I knew things were different. They'd been changed. I'd been changed. I hadn't done anything. I hadn't touched the woman beyond that innocent finger at my ear. I'd left before she ended the next song. It was old, something I'd never heard before, Gaelic or Scottish, one word crashing and rolling into the next, each of them lilting upward. Her voice beckoned, and her eyes. She never took them off me. Not once. Not even as I was walking out the door.

I'd wanted to go back, wanted to fall into her music, to let her fingers play along my hair. Mostly I'd wanted to hear her, that sea-shelled voice in my ear as she dug her fingers into me. As she came. But I didn't. I wouldn't.

I had barely fallen asleep before Michelle was up, wanting to talk, wanting to make things right. As she talked, I found much of my anger had slipped away. Fear, shame, guilt. These were all that I had left.

"What did you do last night?" She finally asked the question that had been in her eyes since she opened them. She was hesitant to touch me, keeping her fists curled softly at her sides.

"Oh." I couldn't look at her and I slid from the sheets, talking away from her. "I saw this woman last night, this singer. She was fantastic." I talked about her voice and the music while I tried to spoon coffee into the tiny hotel coffee maker. Grounds were spilling all over, sticking to my skin.

"Sounds great," she said, pulling herself from bed and coming to wrap her arms around me. "Let's go and see her tonight. I'm taking the day off. I need it."

And suddenly, I didn't want to share her. I didn't want to hear Michelle take her apart note-by-note. "See, that's a c-sharp and it should have been a g-flat," or "Now, when she's a second behind the beat like that..." What? Did I think I was going to have an affair with the pub singer? Maybe. I think it was more than that. Something that I had that was all mine. I didn't have a job, or a house. I wasn't even painting. But she made me want to paint again, and that was something I wanted to hold on to.

Michelle was watching me expectantly, her dark eyes meeting mine in the mirror, a hand trailing along the curve of my thigh.

"She was probably a one-time thing," I said. "Down at the dive bar, near Marion."

Michelle stood on her tiptoes and nipped at the side of my neck and a dark shudder wove up through me, like a vine wrapping tightly around my insides. "Oh, I haven't been there yet. Come on. It'll be fun."

I flicked the coffee maker on with a click, watching my own movements, unable to raise my gaze into her eyes. "Fine."

"Great," she said. She turned me away from the mirror and slowly sank down in front of me, her shoulder muscles bunching beneath the skin as she brushed her lips down my stomach. She spread my legs with her hands and then curled her tongue into the heat of me, her dark eyes laughing as she looked up. I closed my eyes, arched into her glossy stroke. And I imagined it was her, singing to me, singing songs deep into the bones of me, into the sinew and muscle, until my blood beat in tune to the graveled, husky shore of her voice.

———————◆———————

I didn't mean to crash. But I was so tired, and we'd been up all day, Michelle apologizing about the baby thing, and me saying, "Shhh, it's okay," even though something had hardened inside me like fossil, like stone. A tiny bit of me that knew, even then, that there was an end in our future.

And in the end, I slept. Michelle went out. Not to find her, she says. She says that still. Just to go out. But that's where she ended up. Sometimes now when I look back, I wonder. Did she suspect something all along? Or did she just end up, like me, enthralled, entranced, dragged there against her will? Why else didn't she wake me? Why else didn't she take me with her?

I've pieced it together in my mind, what happened, although Michelle's never said. I lay in bed while Michelle walked to the bar, early evening. Maybe had a drink. Catching her croon from down the street, already dissecting it with her trained ear and brain. I could see Michelle sitting there, a drink in her hand, cocking her head, her foot beating in time to the tunes, her dark eyes on the sway of hips. What did she sing to Michelle, I wonder now, still.

What did she croon to wrap her inside a dark cocoon?

I woke up late, the evening long gone and the dark night fallen, my head swimming with images of spiraling hips, songs-upon-songs that I followed but couldn't find. I ended up at the water's edge, its dark seep covering my bare toes in muck and grime, pinning me there.

"Chelle?" But I knew before I spoke that I was alone in the room. And I knew, even without knowing, where she'd gone.

Michelle wasn't at the bar. Neither was the singer. But somehow, I knew where I'd find them. I followed my half-dream, let it lead me to the edges of the city, my feet not bare but knowing the route nonetheless. Down to where there was nothing but dirty water and broken pieces. And when I heard her voice, its voice, not the smoked-out, glass-edged honky tonk from the other night, but a high, sweet, pitch-perfect note, I knew.

I came over the rise, stepped onto the low edge where the lap of water was still too high, too fast. In the almost-moon, I could see them: Michelle, her skin glistening in dirt-water and meager moonlight, buried beneath the singer's body, the way she crawled over Michelle on hands and knees, alligator, serpent. Their bodies so entwined, I could only watch while she bent her head to Michelle's ear, whispered something that made Michelle's body bridge upward off the sand. Pulsing. Michelle's head turned my way, so that if her eyes weren't pulled shut from pleasure, she would have seen me standing there. One brief flash, I imagined myself painting this: The singer. Michelle. Me.

Then a low moan of desire – I knew that sound, a sound like no other, even if I didn't have the technical terms for it, the way to describe its tempo and beat – rose from Michelle's throat. It tore my breath out of my chest, sent my knees tumbling to the wet muck beneath me.

I waited until I could almost hitch a breath, still watching, unable to close my eyes. If I go back to that moment and stay there, just a moment longer, I can tell myself that I didn't know what that creature was or what she wanted, the way she'd lured and captured, spun her watery web around us both. I tell myself I would have fought for Michelle. But that's not the truth. Pushing myself up slow, like a child learning to walk, I turned away. I would have left Michelle there. I meant to leave her there.

It was the creature who let her go, spit her out as fast as she'd wrapped her up, leaving Michelle still and closed-eyed, as though she was far in sleep, dreaming. The creature raised its reflective blue eyes to mine, let them rest there a long time. A soft laughing hiss that could have been waves or the wind through stones or my own breath curled up through my ears. The stench of bog water rose in my nostrils, the reek of creatures giving birth among the dead, and I gagged. Slowly, it moved back, disappearing into the darkness of the water. And still, when the notes came, as I knew they would, as jagged and cigarette-sucked as they were before, I wanted to follow them, to spiral down and down in it, to let it wash over me and drown me in its sound.

———◆◆◆———

We've been inland for six months now. I'm painting again. Giant canvases that fill the living room, muddied and blurred. They sell for a good amount of money and earn me praise like, "Ahead of her time" and "Up-and-coming queer artist." I use a lot of grays and browns and greens. The critics ask me what I'm trying to say about my experiences as a lesbian or what demons I'm trying to expel, and I know I look at them funny. I can't tell them the truth. I'm not trying to expel any demon. I'm trying to get it back.

Michelle stopped working when she got sick. The doctors are seeing what it is. They thought cyst. Now they think tumor. But I know better. I know that it's neither of those things. Not the way Michelle is in the morning, not the way her skin has turned rosy, or the way her stomach would feel beneath my hands if I could bear to touch it. I know it's an egg from her, filling her. The gift that should have been mine.

I won't be here much longer. I'm waiting. With my hands on a brush and my ears always craning to hear. I'm listening for the song of death or the keen of birth, whichever comes for me first. Some days I don't know which one I'm wishing for.

STORY NOTES FOR
THE LURE OF DANGEROUS
WOMEN

When I came up with the idea for "Trill," I was living in a friend's flat on a nine-mile-long island in Scotland. It was spring, I could see the ocean from my bedroom, I was going through a divorce, and I had just been bitten by a tick carrying Lyme disease. For more than two weeks, I lay in a brass bed next to the ocean and knew I was dying.

At the end of two weeks, I was pretty sure I wasn't dying anymore, but I was sick and angry and scared. I couldn't write because my wrists sang with glass shards every time I moved them. I couldn't read because my eyes were not working properly. I couldn't have sex or an orgasm because the antibiotics were wreaking such havoc on my body. So I lay beneath the covers in a fever dream and I wrote brainstories. In one of those stories, I called my body a "burnt-out house." In another, I traced the origin of the werewolf race. And in "Trill," I scared myself as hard as I could. Then I imagined an ending that scared me even more, an ending that I knew I would never write.

It was another two and a half months before I felt well enough to rise and venture down the circular stairs of my flat. I sat next to the ocean and wrote "Trill" in one sitting. Writing it, I scared myself again. And I put in the real, true ending, even though I knew it meant the story would probably never get published.

I sent the story to a contest by Anthology Builder, and to my shock, "Trill" won first place. Despite the judges' comments that the ending made them so uncomfortable that they almost didn't want to place it.

Every time I read "Trill," I wonder where that horror came from. And then I remember those weeks, when I was sure I was dying, and I have my answer.

———◦●◦———

"Seed" is a shower story. I have shower stories and long walk stories and doing dishes stories. They come at me, lightspeed, and ask me why I haven't written them yet. It is difficult to explain that I haven't written them because I didn't know about them, but they are unhappy hearing that and usually badger me until I leave what I'm doing and go get my laptop.

When "Seed" arrived to pester me, I had just moved back to Portland, Oregon after a long and writingless stint in Dallas, Texas. I was living with some friends, essentially renting out a room and a bathroom, and sharing a communal living room and kitchen. While in the shower, I starting thinking about the things we keep private: mostly bodily functions like self-cleaning, sleep, and sex. Yet we eat together, an act that is in some ways a bodily function and is in many ways far more intimate.

Later that same day, the three of us were eating ripe, perfect peaches in the kitchen, the juice dripping down our arms, wiping our mouths with the back of our hands, moaning in pleasure at the taste of such edible perfection.

So I started thinking what it would mean if eating became the new sex. If eating was considered a thing to do in private, a shamed thing. Would you get embarrassed if you ate in front of someone? Would it be different if you ate a piece of hard candy versus a ripe, juicy, dripping peach? Would people pay for the pleasure of watching you eat? What would the social ramifications be of someone who wantonly ate in front of others, who invited others back to their kitchens, who broke bread with a stranger? Would there be repercussions if someone forced you to eat against your will, essentially raped you with food?

But a story isn't a story for me until I have a character, an image, a voice in my head. "Seed" didn't come to life until I saw a man buying cherries at the local farmers' market. I watched as he fed them slowly, one by one, to the woman he was with. And in that instant, I had both the narrator of my story, and the catalyst.

When I was eighteen, I fell in love with a boy who spent his nights saving lives and fighting fires.

He could never drink at parties because he was on call, but he would come back after emergencies smelling of smoke and sweat, telling the most amazing stories. It wasn't long after that I joined the ambulance and fire crew. (This is a trend, by the way. Most of my skills throughout life I've learned because I fell in love or lust with someone – scuba diving, motorcycle riding, volleyball, role-playing games, wine-tasting, cooking, sailing).

Eighteen is very young for saving lives. The experience changed me fundamentally in ways that I wouldn't understand until many years later. I wrote a series of poems about it, as well as a bad novel (unpublished) and a dark story ("Forced Expiration"). I just couldn't let the experience go. It was like I was driven to keep mining it until I got to the nugget of how it changed me.

When I sat down to write a story for an anthology with a theme of "taking flight," a bunch of disparate elements came together to form "Seeing Stars": someone famous had just died from auto-asphyxiation and it was all over the news, I was working on compiling my paramedic poems into a book, and my friend had recently taken a helicopter ride and told me all about it. I wanted to tell a story in which the main character does her job very well – the needles and the bag and the proper medical distance – but who doesn't truly understand what she's doing on an emotional, human level. At least, not at the beginning. But every experience and interaction changes us, even if we resist it.

I wrote "Animal Instincts" while walking the Scottish shoreline. I was recovering from Lyme disease and trying to get my strength back. So I walked and listened to the ocean hitting the land and thought about crossing over water to the land of the dead. I was doing research on psychopomps (creatures who are responsible for escorting newly deceased souls to the afterlife) for another story and mulling over how they seemed to me both scary and comforting.

I'd grown up on a farm, and every year we raised pigs (a common psychopomp) for meat. All year long, we fed them table scraps and scratched their bellies and made them into very happy, very fat pigs. When it was time to take them to the butcher, we lured the them on to the truck with the grain-in-pail technique, offering up yummy food and calling them sweetly by their names so they wouldn't get stressed out on the trip. Which, in an odd kind of way, made me something of a psychopomp to the pigs.

It was the image of a pig with its head in a bucket, nosing around for something tasty, that really brought the ending of this story home for me. I wrote it in one sitting, and was bawling and shivering by the time I wrote the last scene. I couldn't eat apples for weeks.

———◆◆◆◆———

"One-Woman Town" is the most recent story in this collection. In the fall of 2011, I was doing regular write-ins with writer Mary Robinette Kowal at a local coffee shop. We would meet, write for 45 minutes, talk for 15 minutes, and then repeat the process until we either couldn't stand ourselves anymore or the coffee shop closed. It was a very productive system for me. I don't remember where I got the idea for this story, but I do remember those days stretching out before me, coffee in hand, laptop on the table, fall sun coming through the windows, knowing I couldn't get up until I'd written for 45 minutes. I had just ended a bad relationship, and I was thinking about love and heartbreak and how we hurt each other in the act of trying to love each other. We all do it. Some of us just do it in worlds where magic and song and robots make it so much easier to do damage.

"Forced Expiration" was the first dark story I ever wrote. I had just read this brilliant story called "Fuck Dying," by Maggie Grey, which is about a woman whose volunteer work is to bring sexual pleasure to those who are dying. The story is fantastic and heart-breaking and sexy, and the premise really caught me. I kept rereading the story and thinking, "Wow. What if our country actually understood the importance of such a thing? What if they not only allowed sex as a healing treatment, but encouraged it and even included it as part of our insurance packages?" I rolled that idea around in my brain for a long time and then sat down to write something based on that premise.

As often happens for me, the characters emerged fast and furious and wanted to do their own things. And it got very complicated as well. The narrator is doing her job, doing what she knows is the right thing for the patient. And she is paid to be there. But her work still isn't accepted. Not by the other nurses, not by the hospital, not even by the patients whose lives she saves. Still, she continues on, driven only by the belief that her actions are important.

It was a long time after I wrote this story that I realized it was really a story about writing, about how we go on, despite not having the support of those around us, because we also believe our actions are important, that every story can make a difference.

———◆◆◆———

The first time I went to New Orleans, it was pre-Katrina. I landed in the city to begin a cross-country road trip. We had one night and one day in New Orleans before we left for our next destination. I mostly remember a lot of naked women, sweat, deep-fried pickles, and sleeping in a hotel room with seven guys, tucked on the floor between the bed and the window, hoping that no one would roll over on me in the middle of the night.

The second time I went to New Orleans, it was for the Saints and Sinners festival. I mostly saw the inside of a conference center.

The third time I went was for another road trip, this one from Portland to New York. It was post-Katrina. Our hotel was the same hotel that's in the story, and my partner and I walked together to a tiny, nondescript bar around the corner. There we saw this fantastic singer. Her voice was pure gravel and blues, yet clear and sweet as water. She was living music, her body, her movements, the dress that shimmied around her. I couldn't take my eyes off her. Surely she was a siren, a thing brought from another world.

During her first break, she worked the crowd, collecting tips in a small plastic cup. She worked her way toward me, almost as directly as if she'd known, and tucked her tip cup behind her, making it impossible to reach. Then she leaned in and put her finger at the very bottom edge of my ear, somehow blocking out all ambient noise, and she asked, "What would you like?"

I can't even remember what I answered, if I answered at all. I was flustered, enamored, aroused, and certain that I'd just been touched by a creature from another place. I couldn't stop thinking about her. Oddly, my partner didn't have the same experience, and was rather nonplussed about both her singing and my insistence that she was otherworldly. She ended up in this story because I had to capture her on paper so she wouldn't slip away, back to the waters from whence she came.

ABOUT THE AUTHOR

Shanna Germain claims the titles of writer, editor, leximaven, vorpal blonde, she-devil, and Schrödinger's brat. Her stories, essays, poems, and novellas have appeared in hundreds of anthologies and magazines, including *Absinthe Literary Review, Best American Erotica, Best Erotic Romance, Pank, Salon,* and *Storyglossia.* An Associate Fellow at the Attic Institute in Portland, OR, she has taught classes in writing, publishing, media, and photography at a wide variety of places. She's even garnered an award here and there, including a Pushcart nomination, the Rauxa Prize for Erotic Poetry and the C. Hamilton Bailey Poetry Fellowship.

Visit her wild world of words online at *www.shannagermain.com.*

Want to read more?

For something fantastical and sultry, try *Beneath Sea & Sky: Erotic Stories of Fantasy,* www.amazon.com/Beneath-Sea-Sky-Stories-ebook/dp/B005NRQNM4.

For something sweet and sexy, try *Safe Haven,* www.amazon.com/Safe-Haven-Xcite-Romance-ebook/dp/B0086G6NJ2.

For passionate, edgy erotica, try the *Bound by Lust* anthology, with stories collected and edited by Shanna. www.amazon.com/Bound-Lust-Submission-Sensuality-ebook/dp/B0081RLI3C.

www.ingramcontent.com/pod-product-compliance
Lightning Source LLC
Chambersburg PA
CBHW022034170626
46808CB00003B/1191